BENEATH THE DARK

IAN BACKHOUSE

CRANTHORPE
—MILLNER—
PUBLISHERS

First published by Cranthorpe Millner Publishers (2022)

ISBN 978-1-80378-033-7 (Paperback)

www.cranthorpemillner.com

Cranthorpe Millner Publishers

For my beautiful wife
Lou
Who literally saved my life

And a huge thank you to Rob
- you know why

But the way of the wicked is like total darkness
They have no idea what they are stumbling over

Proverbs 4:19

Have nothing to do with the fruitless deeds of darkness

Ephesians 5:11

PROLOGUE

It knew itself that it was living, but was not alive. Even more so now it could sense the acute and potent energy flowing down. Raw instinct drew it towards the source of the power. A power which effervesced from an abundance of sources that had begun to materialise and conjoin, triggering an innate, irreversible compulsion to peel and wrench and tear itself up and away from its primeval roots towards it.

Life.

Sentience.

Self.

It did not understand how, but it could feel the acute force, calling it up from the depths and knew it offered such.

Offered what it must never have.

Offered it the antithesis of its own reason for existence.

And as it tore away from its stems, began moving closer to that intoxicating energy, for the first time it understood its own malevolence, the unfathomable depth of its own cruelty.

And as it continued to move towards the source, if it could have smiled, it would have done so...

Late Summer, 1996

ONE

Frank Bernie was no snowflake - eighteen years in the Parachute Regiment, fourteen years in private security after that, retiring at fifty-eight. He was still able to get out of a chair without the involuntary grunt that usually accompanied men of his age and he had kept his mind sharp.

Which was why in the semi-darkness, he'd found himself so dumbfounded, felt the dribble trickle down the inside of his leg, the punch of terror in his stomach so hard that he'd staggered backwards into one of the glass displays. His heavy bulk had bounced off the reinforced glass, and he'd thrust his arms out, grasping for anything that might be there to steady himself, only finding thin air, and a hard drop to the floor.

Oddly enough, the afternoon had started very well. Bright sunshine and a cloudless sky, the muted cry of gulls, people passing by, occasional laughter drifting in through the narrow ticket hall.

He'd purchased the small museum on the seafront a month ago, combining his retirement plan to live by the sea with owning a small local business. All his life he'd been a runner. It was his passion, and although now his distance and pace were far gentler, it was his one way of escaping everything. No matter what was going on in his life, running had always been the one thing that took him to a peaceful place, and the ability to now run on the beach every day was the realisation of a lifelong goal.

A steady trickle of visitors had continued, including the odd young man the day before, who had spent almost two hours wandering around, eventually buying a replica ration book, map, and a hardback about the English civil war. He'd seen him before along the seafront. A local, possibly, rather than a tourist, though they were beginning to dwindle now the late summer was coming to an end.

He closed dead on time as the darkening evening started to persuade beach lovers to pack up and head for the pubs and restaurants, stopping for a moment before locking the main entrance, enjoying the view. The horizon was a thin strip of white light under orange-stained clouds, the shore a dark mass, featureless now, the sound of the distant tide the only thing to prove its presence.

It was peaceful.

Tranquil -

- until the sound of detonating glass suddenly shattered the silence.

He turned sharply, but instead of rushing in to

investigate, he held his ground, listening. Even now, his years in a caution-dependant career kept his fight or flight response sharp.

Silence…

Just the waves in the distance.

Stealthily he closed the door, but left it unlocked. He'd already switched all the display cabinet lights off, leaving on just the rows of ceiling LEDs that ran throughout the museum, casting double reflections and deep shadows across the contents of each cabinet. Most of the artefacts in them were small and eclectic: letters home from soldiers, Roman pottery, Victorian toys, pre-war mariners' equipment, historic farm apparatus – an odd collection documenting the island's unusual history. There were also several cabinets throughout the museum in which mannequins told the story. And though he'd have never admitted it to anyone, Frank always found them a little creepy in the half-light when shutting up shop. None of your lip-trembling or knee-shaking kind of nonsense, just a little uneasiness. Their facial features seemed to melt away, and if he stared long enough for his eyes to distinguish shape from shadow, he always thought he could suddenly see a mouth or eye begin to move. Clearly an illusion, but enough to cause his pace to quicken ever so slightly as he passed those particular cases.

No further noise came, so, softly, he began walking along the entrance hall, catching sight of his reflection, sliding from glass pane to glass pane of each display. A hint of paunch was visible, but for a man of his age, he had an upright gait, reasonable musculature, and the suit he wore sat well on him.

He listened again, still walking. It was difficult to tell where the sound of the breaking glass had come from – the small rooms and corridors with their low ceilings and rough plastered walls caused sounds to behave oddly. The museum had originally been a medieval wool house, and even now, the beams and ironwork emitted a mild, musty odour, lending the place an additional eccentricity.

As he moved along the entrance hall toward the Roman room, he thought it unlikely to be one of the cabinets. They were safety glass. Which just left the windows. Some nasty little thief trying his luck? Well, he'd show them the business end of an ex-para's training.

The entrance hall curved gently to the right, and as he reached the doorway to the Roman room, placing a soft footstep on to the tiled floor, the entire row of ceiling lights flickered erratically -

- then died –

- plunging him into darkness.

He stopped, immediately shut his eyes for a few seconds. When he opened them his night vision had kicked in and he could at least make out the boundaries of the room, and the black, yawning rectangle to his left – the entrance to the Victorian room. So, the amateur thought cutting a couple of wires was going to scare him?

Then the same sound fragmented the silence again, the shattering of glass, now so much louder.

His heart wanted to leap into his throat, but self-control refused to allow such a reaction. His head instinctively turned towards the sound, the corridor to the left. Clearly nothing was going on in the room he now stood in. Once again, he began to move forward, still softly, still slowly, towards the dingy doorway.

And as he passed through it, the vague shapes emerging in the mirk, a single ceiling LED flickered back on, horribly dim, doing little to make the room any more inviting.

He frowned – so the electrics hadn't been cut. On the left and right were wall-to-ceiling, glass-fronted displays. The left told the story of industry on the island during the late 1800s – manual mining equipment, small medical implements, textile sample – and two mannequins: a local 'gent' of the day, and a chimney sweep. The local 'gent' had been rescued from a tip, a haggard specimen, one missing eye roughly painted back in, a crack running down the cheek and no bottom lip. The lack of light cast deep pockets of shadow across its face, making it appear oddly distorted. The chimney sweep was a boy, face smothered in boot polish for soot, bare feet, and a threadbare brush clumsily nailed to one of his hands. His white eyes were all the more obvious for the polish across his brow and cheeks, as they stared sightlessly towards the floor in the middle of the room.

In the centre of the room was a column display, housing just the one mannequin, a soldier of the Royal Northumberland Fusiliers – black peaked hat, bright red waist tunic, and dark blue trousers gathered over black boots.

Finally, there was the main piece, a display that went floor to ceiling and the entire width of the room opposite the entrance. If he did say so himself, Frank thought this the most authentic exhibit in the museum, a mock-up of a Victorian nursery. There was a cast-iron fireplace on the left wall, and a high bookshelf on the right. Between these was a wicker table and two small chairs covered in toys of the period: a china tea set, teddy bears, alphabet building blocks, chequers board, a large doll's house, circular train set, rocking horse, tin drum and more. The scene was almost completed by the mannequin of the nanny holding the pram at the very back, as if about to leave for a gentle wander around one of the island's parks, dressed in a black French twill dress from neck to ankle, there was no white apron as was sometimes worn. Nothing to lift the dourness. Severity, commitment, and discipline exuded from her. Her face was obscured by a black bonnet, and even standing to the far left or right of the display, her face always seemed to remain just out of vision. The carriage pram was also black, set in a dark wood frame with a folding hood, curled handle, and spoked wheels, and peeking over the side of the pram was one of the two hundred and thirty-two exhibits that truly completed the entire scene. They lined the front of the display, sat on every available surface, dressed in a bewildering array of styles, some on the knees of others, the smaller ones propping up some of the larger ones –

Dolls.

Four hundred and sixty-four over-sized, unsighted eyes, set above gaudy rouge cheeks painted on glazed, yellowing skin staring out at nothing.

He looked about – certainly no damage to the displays. He turned to the Fusilier. The glass looked intact. Both times the smashing of glass had sounded so loud and violent. But so far, there was nothing to suggest any such occurrence in the rooms he'd passed through. He shook his head, turned back to the nursery display again. It *had* to be a window. These cabinets were virtually indestructible. All part of health and safety these days. So that meant going through to the kitchen area at the rear of the building – the only room with windows.

But he still had to take it carefully – what if the intruder had already got in? He didn't want to rush on through only to meet him coming the other way. He needed to keep the advantage, stay stealthy and slow. So, he moved off again, keeping to the left edge of the side displays. As dim as the single ceiling-light was, he missed its glow instantly as he moved into the gloom again towards the nursery at the end of the room.

He stopped a couple of feet before he reached the doorway that would take him through the next two rooms and into the kitchen. He glanced across at the nanny – now just a flat shape in the darkness, still gripping the carriage pram. Disconcertingly, weak shreds of light still managed to pick out sporadic faces of the dolls that surrounded her, each gazing off in a different direction. Still, it didn't look like anything was damaged there either.

He listened again for any sounds that might indicate someone was now inside the building. But needn't have bothered.

It sliced through the silence yet again, the detonation of splintering glass erupting from immediately behind him. He spun, coming face to face with the Fusilier –

- still encased and inanimate.

Then from his left and right simultaneously as if the cases were bursting open down each side of the room, the sound came again. His jaw gaped as again, nothing happened before him, just that deafening sound.

Then from behind him - shattering glass again.

He whirled, what was left of the single LED dimmed and died, and he threw up his arms as the pane before the nursery display blew out, the noise searing his eardrums! In that split-second, he waited for the sting of flying splinters to lacerate exposed skin – but no pain came. He dropped his arms slowly, revealing to himself the unbroken glass before him. He stared at it, then took a step forward, eyes never leaving the display. Then another step, and one more, fingertips reaching out to touch the pane tentatively. It didn't yield, and he pressed harder, began running his palms across it.

No cracks.

Smooth.

Unblemished.

Slowly he brought the tip of his nose within an inch of the glass. His peripheral vision faded as he fixed his gaze on the dolls, all of them still staring off blindly at random angles into the dark. He lifted his eyes up to the inky form of the nanny, still holding on to the pram.

Nothing else in there.

No one else in there.

He stole a glance left.

Then right.

Then back at the dolls –and every head had turned, all of them now staring sightlessly at him.

Yet before he could scream, his head snapped up as the nanny came hurtling through the air towards him with a detestable, shrill shriek from her long gaping mouth, as if the jaw itself were melting downward. The twill dress flailed, her arms flat at her sides, the rest of her face featureless as it slammed into the glass an inch from his –

- which was when he'd recoiled in abject terror, bounced off the Fusiliers cabinet and hit the floor, cracking the side of his head on the skirting, where he now found himself laying.

For a second or two, he saw white flecks darting across his vision, but terror took over, and he was up on his knees, scrambling backwards, then pushing himself up on to his feet to meet that hideous oncoming nanny —

- nothing.

All of the ceiling-lights were back on. The nursery display was exactly as it always was.

There was silence.

At which point he realised he'd wet himself, and the gush of warm blood down the back of his balding scalp made him shiver. His whole body was trembling. Without a second thought he made for the kitchen area, steadying himself against walls and cabinets along the way, legs flailing like a new-born calf, blood spattering to the floor. He no longer cared if anyone else was in the building. Almost wished there was - anything but being alone here, now. Reaching the Prehistoric room, he as much as collapsed through the door marked 'Staff' at the far-left corner, and fell into the kitchen, saving his balance on one of the work units.

Catching his breath, he looked around desperately, seeing the hot-cupboard. He grabbed it, using his full weight to pull it into motion, and forced it up against the door. At least in the Paras, he fought an enemy he could *see*. This was insane!

His trembling was now uncontrollable, the blood from his wound flooding down underneath his shirt and across his back. He stumbled over to check the windows were locked and dropped the blinds. Snatching up the phone from the wall, he stabbed at it, getting Jon's number right after the third shaky attempt. Raising it to his ear, he waited for the ring at the other end.

The line buzzed gently. A few seconds more, he thought.

It continued to buzz.

And buzz...

...and then he let out a long sigh, as the ring tone began.

And rang...

...and rang...

"Come on Jon, please, please answer the damn phone."

A few more seconds and at last, the 'click' of the receiver being lifted at the other end.

"Hello, Jon?"

"Hello, Jon?" His own voice echoed back at him.

"Jon?"

"Jon?" His own voice again.

"Can you hear me?"

"Can you hear me?"

"Oh, for Christ's sake!"

"Don't curse, Frank. Your mother raised you better than that," his own voice told him.

The phone flew from his hand, the coiled wire too long to save it from smashing open on the tiled floor. He grabbed a chair, pulling it to the opposite corner of the room and behind the tall catering shelf. He slumped into it, back to the wall staring at the door, eyes wide and watery. Blood immediately beginning to soak into the back of the chair. The piss on his trousers was starting

15

to smell, but he didn't even notice; he wasn't going anywhere. He was going to sit right here until daylight.

Until Maureen turned up to clean the place.

Lovely, normal Maureen.

Whom he could see.

Whom he could touch.

Who was real.

TWO

The Black Dog was the most popular pub on the island, both for the locals and tourists. It was built in 1284 as a house for the landowner, the rather unpopular The Baron de Fray, Edward Lambton, rather fitting then, that after his string of crimes against the population of the island, and his ill-disguised hatred for any place that wasn't landlocked, he'd drowned when the boat taking him back to the mainland sank.

It was constructed from island stone, with square double windows at the front, gable roof with loft window, and a stubby, three-tiered chimney. To the far right was the original entrance to the kitchens, and remained so, whilst the far left, a head-bumping five-foot doorway offered entry to the main bar. The 13th-century flagstones led from the entrance through the expansive garden that ended at the cliffs, a beautiful view overlooking the shore. At sunset, the punters doubled in number, all eyes on the apricot haze, drinks in hands.

Inside, the bar, made from the same stone as the

building, ran the length of the room, curving to the wall at the end by the entrance to the small restaurant section. An extensive choice of gins, rums, local bottled brews, and some rather unusual spirits adorned the rear wall. Photographs hung on most of the walls: the moorland, the town on The Borrow and houses on The Lend, the original steam locomotive that connected the two across The Horseshoe and others – authentic depictions of the island's history. The furnishings were generous and comfortable, with two and three-seater sofas, armchairs by the fireplace and a couple of stools at the bar.

Early afternoon had brought with it a powder blue sky with high, mackerel clouds. A few tourists remained on the island, but in a couple of weeks they'd be gone. Angus Ferris, owner and landlord, made his money during the high season with no difficulty, so the quiet months were not an issue. In fact, they were a welcome rest, if he was asked.

Jon had decided to drop in, more to check up on Clara than anything. He and Angus had been good mates for more than fourteen years. Jon had been the island bobby for the last twenty-two, initially Angus's contact for anything to do with licensing, and they'd hit it off pretty much straight away. The landlord felt that his own no-nonsense approach to life had had much to do with their smooth alliance at first, Jon himself not coming across as a man to suffer fools gladly either. Of course, there had been plenty of times when Jon had been there to help him roust the occasional meat-head or pathetic herd of knuckle-draggers during high season. His daughter, Clara, had started working in the pub with him, taking a break before beginning her PhD in the spring. Unfortunately, the day before, she'd had a run-in with a pair of mainlanders who'd come over to try and sell cheap weed. They'd tried to rob her, and she'd given one of them a bloody nose, but got shoved hard into a wall the second before they ran off. Angus had picked her up and was adamant that Jon needn't come out, so he thought he'd drop in to see how she was.

"Civies? Day off?" Angus asked.

"I wish. Coke please, mate."

"Push the boat out," Angus smiled.

As the landlord turned to grab a can from the back fridge, Jon caught sight of himself in the etched mirror that stretched the length of the bar: a middle-aged man, with steel-grey hair cut an inch short to the scalp. His face, weathered but still strong, gave the impression of dependability. At 6ft, he'd kept his weight healthy over the years, something he knew was essential for his job.

Angus passed him the can.

"Ta. So, how's Clara?" Jon asked, opening his drink, and taking a swig.

"She's fine. She's at the cash and carry, back in about half an hour. You know what she's like. Won't put up with any shit from anyone, no matter who they are or how big they are."

Jon smirked inoffensively. "She's had a good role model. Was she hurt?"

"Bruise on her back, but nothing serious. Cowards."

"We won't be seeing too many of that type much longer, mate. The ferry's dropping to three trips a day from next week, now the seasons coming to an end, remember? Just your usual pain-in-the-arse customers to worry about soon." He had a quick look around – "like him," he finished nodding towards Kyle Watts, the island's labourer, and handyman. Kyle gave him the finger with a laugh. Jon raised his can to him and smiled.

He'd clocked the rest of the clientele as he'd walked in. There were just three other customers, all locals: Harry Rigby, a retired pharmacist at the far end of the bar, Bryce Edwards, the town's solicitor by the unlit fire, and Roger Bremman, one of two farmers on the island.

Angus drew Jon's attention back to him. "Always the copper. Do you ever just go into a pub, sit down and have a drink without scouting the place out first?"

"Don't realise I'm even doing it most of the time. And talking of bad habits, when are you gonna get rid of that hideous beard?"

Angus stroked his copious whiskers, feigning hurt. "It's called style."

"It's called 'dirty trawler-man'."

"Sod off," Angus said.

Jon slipped from his stool, laughing quietly, and made his way over to Kyle who sat on one of the two-seater sofas by the window.

"How are you doing, Kyle?" he asked, sitting down.

The well-built young man in a baggy Iron Maiden t-shirt and ropey looking jeans nodded. "Checking up on me again?"

"You know me. Can't leave things alone."

Kyle gave a wry smile. "I'm fine, Jon."

"No issues with accommodation anymore?"

"All good. Once you'd had a word, the Accommodation Board backed off. The landlord was more than happy to have me. Nice bloke. Takes people as he finds them." He took a sip of his bitter.

"So how's work going?"

"Still there." Kyle wasn't exactly the touchy-feely type, but Jon knew he appreciated his help. And he told Kyle he'd do it again. It wasn't about being appreciated – it was about fair play, a bit of decent justice in a shitty world.

Kyle was, at the core, a good man. He just seemed to have a lot of bad luck. And Jon had not been about to let a clear case of self-defence get twisted by some silver-spooned QC. The police officer had commended Kyle on the gargantuan size of his nads for bringing in the wounded youth (leading to the other four getting nicked), knowing he'd likely be arrested for assault as well.

He heard the main door open and heard a sigh from Kyle as Ernest Gibson shuffled in. He regarded Angus, saw the look of antipathy in his eyes. The landlord was a hefty build, muscle losing the battle with cellulite though - just a little. His dark, swept-back hair, thick but neat, clashed oddly with his red beard and 'tash, making him look like a character from 'The Beano', according to his daughter. Such features, along with his name, were regularly responsible for people assuming him to be Scottish: he was from Croydon - though he did have to admit to having a Glaswegian great-grandfather.

Never seen out of a pair of Craghopper cargo shorts, and a Tattersall shirt, regardless of season, he was a grafter, always had been, something instilled in him from an early age by his father. And although a man who was plain speaking, and invariably opinionated, for the most part, he was quietly spoken.

"What can I get you, Ernest?" he asked flatly.

"Stout." The old man fished around in a small leather purse, produced the coins, and dropped them onto the bar. A muffled curse came from the rear of the room. Angus ignored it. Jon looked around and saw Roger Bremman wiping beer froth from his lips with a forearm catching Jon's eye and immediately looking away. The police officer understood where Roger was coming from but nothing had ever been proved. It was all rumour. Something a small island community lent itself to rather readily. No one had ever come forward with an accusation. As far as the law was concerned, there was no proof to suggest that Ernest Gibson was anything other than white as the driven snow. But Jon shared the same gut feelings as many of his friends and colleagues, including Angus and Kyle. The only way he could act on those was to keep a watch on him whenever he could:

which was seldom. Being the only copper on the island meant spreading himself thinly, just to try and keep his head above water. Specimens like Ernest Gibson who deserved his full attention, full investigation, if for no other reason than to rule out any truth to the rumours, walked around with impunity. The law was an ass, but it was the law. Unbelievably he had to wait for some young victim to report being abused by the scumbag before he could do anything concrete – utterly ridiculous. He'd requested additional manpower from HQ on the mainland time after time, but was always turned down. Financial reasons, he was told. Tell that to any victim of Gibson's if they ever came forward.

The pint of stout was put before Gibson, and he pulled himself ineloquently onto a bar stool. His drab, grey clothes looked grubby and greasy, straggly hair scraped thinly across his scalp. He took a sip of his drink, grimy fingers with dirty nails coiled around the glass, then turned his head just enough to meet the stare of each person in the pub, looking from one to the next without a flicker of emotion. Finally, he turned his head back to face the bar wearing a long, neat smile.

Roger Bremman was out of his seat in an instant, almost knocking his table over, striding towards Gibson. Jon shot out a hand as Roger reached his table, grasping his forearm as surreptitiously as he could. Roger paused and looked down at him.

"I'm leaving, that's all," he said, his voice guttural. Jon waited for a second, then released his grip. The farmer made straight for the door, past Gibson without a second glance, and was gone.

There was a silence for some moments, eventually broken by Kyle.

"The rumours about him must go back before my time on the island then, Jon? The guy's a wreck – eighty if he's a day? Wouldn't have thought he's much danger to anyone now."

"To be honest, I can't even remember when it all started. I was a PC then, and it was when my old skipper, Terry Harris, still worked on the island. The fact that it's all stuck around for so many years is the worrying part. 'No smoke', and all that." He stood and emptied his coke can. "Tell you what though, Kyle, I hope to God you're right," he added and returned to the bar.

"Got to get going, Angus. I want to use today to clear the decks as much as I can – I'm planning on a chilled evening: takeaway, bottle of red, phone off the hook and some time to myself."

Angus chucked the can in the bin, moving along to the end beam where he placed his large hand on the wall-phone that had started to ring, pausing before lifting the receiver. "Ok. Take it easy."

Jon walked past Gibson, still sat with a smirk on his face, ignoring him as he reached the door and as he stepped outside, he stood still for a moment, listening to waves far below the cliff. He took a long breath of salt air, tucked in the back of his shirt and wondered why life never seemed to stop being so complicated. Just a pause from all the hassle would be good. A break from the paperwork, and pointless complaints, just for one day would be luxury. About to move off, the shout made him turn.

It was Kyle. "Jon, hold on! The phone - it's for you."

Jon checked his inside pocket and realised he'd left his radio at the nick. He went back inside and found Angus proffering him the phone, consternation on his face. "They've been trying to get hold of you for the last hour," he said. "It's Frank Bernie."

Jon frowned. "What about him?"

"They need you up at the museum straight away."

"Is he ok?"

Angus skewed his jaw. "I think you might want to trash the idea of clearing the decks today," he said, extending his arm fully as Jon came to the bar and took the receiver from him.

THREE

Kyle thought back without alacrity to the conversation he'd had with the police officer earlier, as he walked back along the quiet roads.

He ached from an afternoon putting up 6ft fencing around the new clifftop gardens by himself, and had decided to head straight home. He owed Jon, big time. If it weren't for him, he'd probably still be inside. The police officer understood what had really happened at the Long Mire site. The moor covered a quarter of The Borrow, the east island, the only part that got no visitors, save for land management personnel or the occasional bird watcher. The old rectory was the only remaining building, tucked away at the edge where the trees began to grow again, edging the north coast, miles from the main businesses and tourist attractions that were situated along the seafront.

He was working late at the new drainage site, long after his colleagues had dropped the tools and hit the pub. When the cold had finally started to pinch at him through his several layers, he'd ensconced himself in the main portacabin; couple of blankets underneath and a couple on top, his puffer jacket for a pillow and some tinnies: sorted.

Until the sound of quiet giggles made him sit bolt upright – no one was out here except himself, so the slightest noise seemed magnified and clear. Gravel crunching under feet. Furtive feet. Slow and steady. Were they out to steal plant? There could be no other reason on earth for anyone to be out here, especially at this time of night. He moved to the window, keeping low. Placing the side of his head against the prefabricated wall, not touching the blind, he peered out. His field of vision was limited, but he could see at least one bloke, maybe two. All the arc lights were off, and the only illumination was from a waning moon, sporadic rain clouds not helping.

What now? If he so much as dropped a piece of litter he'd go back inside, but he couldn't let anyone nick stuff. It wasn't the stealing itself: insurance would cover that – it was his job. If they made off with essential gear, the project would go pear-shaped and he'd be out of work. And Jon had put his neck on the line for him for this second chance. The only landline on the site was in the other portacabin which he couldn't get to without being seen. There was no choice, it was up to him.

Quietly slipping out the rear fire door, he peeked around the end of the portacabin with as little of his head showing as possible, saw five blokes strolling through the site.

He bellowed at the top of his voice, trying to keep it deep and confident. "Oi! You lot, get the hell off this site or I'm calling the old bill!" He watched all of them physically jump, heads looking frantically about in all directions, their advantage of surprise now crushed. Then, like lemmings, the first had dashed off to Kyle's far left into the shadows, ducking down behind a stack of plasterboard, each of his mates following one after the other. Kyle found himself stifling a laugh. Idiots. "Yeah, go on, get lost!" he yelled and waited for another reaction.

This time, none came.

He was hoping that being discovered would have frightened them off. No further movement came from behind the plasterboard.

He waited again; couldn't see any of them. After a good five minutes he presumed they'd snuck away, tails between their legs…

…until a second later, when they rushed out of the dark from behind him. The crafty shits had circled round.

He was away on his feet like lightning, streaking across the site, dodging tools, planks, mixers, sending up splatters of mud, as if he'd triggered landmines. He could hear them, jeering, the splash of their feet, as he reached the other portacabin at last. He snatched at the handle – a handle which didn't budge. It was locked. Of course it was. He called himself an idiot, turned to run again but suddenly his fleece was jerked hard and backwards. He stumbled slightly but pivoted around, at once into the boxer's guard.

As the youth before him lost the grip, he snarled, weighing in with a wild haymaker. Way too slow – Kyle's jab had already connected brutally with the edge of his chin, dropping the youth like a sack of cement.

The next yob was already coming in, his sloppy but vicious kick missing Kyle by inches, flat foot slamming up against the portacabin. Kyle took his chance, ducked low and uppercut like a canon, straight into the youth's groin. The scream echoed across the site. It was enough of a shock to stall the remaining three who were closing in, allowing Kyle to dart away. He headed for the two diggers parked thirty feet away. Reaching them a few seconds ahead of his pursuers, he managed to duck behind the tracks of the far vehicle. He looked around for something to defend himself with, saw a collection of tools and equipment piled against the hopper. Throwing open the red plastic case on the top of one pile, he hefted out the Paslode cordless nail gun - *God, what was he doing*? But he had no choice. If just two of these thugs got the better of him, he'd get the crap kicked out him - or worse.

A second later, the three remaining youths had caught up, came charging towards him, all of them teeth gritted and fists clenched. Kyle lifted the nail gun, kept it low, and it hissed as he fired three rapid shots. The first missed, but the second and third sent three-inch, zinc hardened nails into the foot of the leading youth, who crumpled into the mud, howling in pain. The two behind him clocked the nail gun and that did the trick. They turned at full pelt, and Kyle watched, relief pouring through him, as their two mates caught up with them, and they disappeared from sight, still running.

He'd looked down at the youth on the ground who was gripping his foot so hard his knuckles were white, crying between gasps of agony with saliva dribbling down his chin.

"I think you and me both are in the shit mate," he'd said, and taking the youth by the collar, had hauled him up. "I hope you like late-night strolls in the countryside," he'd added. "We're going on a long one, and on that foot, it's not gonna be fun for you."

It turned out that group of drunken twenty-somethings had come across from The Lend, the west island, on the train that linked the two. By the time they reached The Borrow, most of the businesses were closed and islanders had returned by the rail link to their homes on The Lend. No-one lived on the east island, and if not a resident, got the ferry back to the mainland. So, apparently they'd decided to wander around, seeing what trouble they could stir up, even if there was no-one else around that they could upset.

He'd been arrested along with the scrote he'd brought in, but the moment Jon arrived for duty and had been briefed, it didn't take long, after a quick interview, before he was released. Lawful self-defence, Jon had said, and had told him - ordered him to the Black Dog to 'recover' from his ordeal.

Yep, he owed Jon.

Big time.

FOUR

John Denver was giving it his all, "Country Roads" blasting out of the CD player. But only because this was, indeed, a country road. Ed's guilty music secret could never be revealed to anyone and driving in the middle of nowhere like this allowed him to bellow along at the top of his voice – a sound he would agree that no other living being should ever have to suffer.

He slowed as he passed the Chorfa Village sign, thanking careful drivers, and fifty feet on, left onto an expansive gravel drive, and turned down the stereo. He carried on through a pair of high iron gates, the faded plaque on the left post telling him he had arrived at Grey Ferns Hall.

Large drops began to slap across his windscreen, lazy and loud, as he cut the engine. He looked up at the ridge of cloud that was bloated black with rain, scudding high over the formidable building before him. Built in the 1830s, Grey Ferns Hall combined Jacobean and Elizabethan styling, beautifully set-off by extensive Baroque massing. Two huge, ornate oriel windows stretched from ground to roof on either side of the building and between them, a large, double oak door guarded the entrance. Above this, a third window commanded wide views of the grounds to the east. Two stacks of twin chimneys crowned each end of the roof, adding yet more grandeur, whilst the base of the property was surrounded by deep flowerbeds, contents now stripped bare by the autumn. Three days he'd been here, and it still never failed to impress him every time he pulled up to it.

He grabbed the carrier-bag from the passenger seat and stepped into the rain, shoes scrunching on the gravel as he jogged to the entrance, then up the stone staircase to the main entrance. Fishing the keys from his pocket, he let himself in, having to push hard against the substantial door. In the entrance hall straight ahead was a large, oak-panelled staircase, stereotypical deer horns and family portraits lining the ascension. The walls were cream, perhaps at one time for the purpose of offsetting the dourness of the wood, but now, dulled by time. Two vast chandeliers, running bulbs now instead of candles, attempted to push back the dim but had little effect despite their size. The floor was of tessellated marble tiles, brown and rust-red, each section bordered in deep blue. An oval walnut drum table graced the centre, hosting an impressive Boulle bracket clock which left space for little else. There were generous doorways opposite each other on the left and right, ancestral marble busts standing sentinel at each door frame. The right led to the Library, the left to the Red Wing past a grand, ten-foot mirror. Ed paused in front of it and began pulling his face around with an index finger. No new spots – how in God's name did a man of forty-six still get spots? His hair was starting to grey, a little wavy, collar length and just the tidy side of shaggy. He kept himself groomed, but without taking it too far – he had to look professional in a job like this to help his credibility. At 5'10" he didn't exactly cut an imposing figure, but he was well-read, principled, and centred, which lent him an air of dependability and stature. Day-to-day, he was a shirt and chinos man, but on a job like this, black polo neck under a fleece and jeans were both warm and practical.

The client, Mrs Evelyn Daphne Harris-Brown – or just Eve, as she insisted on being called, had experienced paranormal events in almost half of the rooms in the building – quite something when you consider there were forty in all. Very unusual in Ed's experience. In places like this, such phenomena tended to be concentrated in one or two rooms. There were exceptions, of course, but not to this degree. The China Boudoir, the White Parlour, the Map Room, the valet's entrance and even the linen room: Eve had seen, heard, or felt something in all twenty. She'd included the list of the rooms in the letter he'd received from her asking for his help. It was this matter-of-fact approach that had caught his attention.

Since his reluctant appearance on a national

television magazine show as part of a Halloween special six years ago (which as a professional debunker, he'd found an odd invitation), requests for his services has quadrupled. Most of his new clients were companies and larger corporations looking for him to 'clear' potential hospitality venues and building projects: a lot of time and money could be wasted by reports from contractors of ghost sightings or supernatural activity, particularly in older building renovations or new builds going up on land associated with urban myths. To many, it sounded ridiculous, but to these companies, it put time-related bonuses and overall profits at huge risk if such disruptions weren't nipped in the bud. Conversely, some clients wanted him to actively prove paranormal activity – country pubs with long histories or rural hotels hoping news of a legitimate haunting would attract a whole new raft of customers. He still took on private cases, as this was his motivation for having started such work in the first place, stemming from a desire to help those who had no-one else to turn to, and up against the fact that no one usually believed them. Even here, he had to tread carefully: separating the genuine requests for help from the fake was not always easy. People could be very convincing on paper. Motives were not always malevolent; people often believed their experiences were real and were convinced they needed expert intervention. Then there were those, of course, who had some kind of angle, some scam that needed a pinch of credibility behind it. He was sure genuine cases had slipped through his fingers at times, but he had to go with his gut instinct, something he'd developed pretty well after twenty-eight years in this line of work.

Eve's letter had been succinct, yet, with an old-world charm. Written in a beautiful hand on quality laid paper, with the list of dates, times and rooms of activity experienced, the request for help had come across as a simple, yet genuine plea from a lady who was accepting of the circumstances, but becoming very tired of its effects. His gut had been right on this one. She was beginning to suffer dizziness, headaches, even nausea.

From the moment he'd arrived, Eve had been the most welcoming and generous client. Regular cups of tea, cake, sandwiches, and an endearing fascination with how he was going about the investigation so, he was not surprised when he reached the West Wing and found a fresh pot of tea and plated biscuits on his monitoring table.

"I'm back, Eve," he called out, dropping the carrier-bag next to the refreshments. He got no reply, but she could be anywhere in this leviathan place. He got on with prepping some of the smaller devices, knowing that eventually she'd come trotting in, pausing at the doorway, taking in all the cameras and mics and sensors with a look of delight. Then her questions would begin.

Ed actually enjoyed her company, which wasn't like him. He worked alone because he didn't trust anyone else to do a good job (as well as not having to complicate any reports with hearsay evidence – any evidence he produced was his, from his own senses and his own equipment), and because he needed complete environmental focus. He didn't find Eve's presence a distraction – it was soothing if anything.

The West Wing was the ideal place to set up the monitoring gear and mobile equipment – or 'mission control' as Eve had decided to name it, which made him smile. It had one door in and out, so any phenomena were more likely to be coming from in front of his position, albeit from other rooms. It made life simpler. It was, compared to most in the building, a small room with windows on just one side so suffered the least noise and light pollution, making monitoring tasks much easier.

The floor was covered with Savonnerie carpets, increasing the absorption of sound, and lessening the chance of erroneous noises that might disrupt any recordings. The walls were hung with royal Gobelins tapestries, again, helping give the whole room an almost 'sound studio' ambience. The only drawback in Ed's opinion was the hideous black and gold panelling that lined the edge of the walls – oppressive and a tad claustrophobic, but hardly the end of the world. He'd investigated places far worse, and this, by comparison, was luxury.

The table at which he now sat was positioned at the back of the room and had six monitors, each with a split-screen covering four cameras. With his back to the wall, he was able to view them and the doorway at the same time. He had his large desk lamp to his left, and audio recording equipment to the right of the monitors. Spare batteries, laser sensors, voice recorders and the like he had stashed on top of the flight cases to the right of the table. A hooded tripod light sat next to these, and together, with the desk lamp, provided just the right amount of illumination to let him see what he was doing without losing too much of his night vision.

As he sat down and started pouring himself a tea, he glanced at the screens to check they were all working correctly and caught sight of Eve as she stood neatly in the doorway, hands together in front of her.

"Knock, knock," she said, smiling. "Did you manage to get my prescription?"

"Indeed I did," Ed replied, fishing it out of the carrier bag.

"That's so kind of you. Thank you."

"Not a problem." Ed came out from behind 'mission control', chomping on a biscuit and joined her, handing her the medication. "How are you feeling now?" He studied her: she was a petite lady of sixty-seven, always immaculately dressed, short silver hair and ruddy complexion, reminding him of someone he might meet in a "Jeeves & Wooster" novel.

"A little unsteady on my feet, and I felt most nauseous this morning. I'm sure that's something you'd rather not hear."

Ed laughed cordially. "Whilst I'm here, there's no reason why I shouldn't help if I can. Hopefully your medication will knock that on the head."

"I've not been allowing myself to be dictated to by it. I'm still walking Harold twice a day now in the fields at the back. Sometimes three. There's a lovely path that runs around it and Harold enjoys the long grass. The exercise helps, you see?" Harold was a fat, eight-year-old pug, who Eve often liked to remind Ed, needed his anal glands expressing more than most other dogs, much to his delight. Having to sometimes lie down on the carpet to set up gear, Ed had since kept a surreptitious eye on Harold in case he caught him in the throes of scooting.

"That's good to hear." He finished his biscuit quickly. "I'm about to do a pre-shift kit inspection if you feel up to joining me again?"

"That would be fascinating, Ed. I shall. But I'll leave you at the east stairs. Early night for me, try and get rid of this bug of mine."

They started to make their way through the rooms. Depending on the phenomena Eve had described in each, depended on what type of equipment Ed had set up. He employed all manner of gadgets - from motion detectors, thermal imaging cameras, night vision cameras, electronic thermometers, voice-activated recorders – all placed very specifically and strategically according to need. Eve asked questions as they went along, clearly intrigued by it all.

As they entered the valet's room, she asked, "Have you ever had a genuine case? One you've been able to prove?"

"Well…I've had cases that I was unable to find any explanation for, scientific or otherwise. Three in the last fifteen years. Some good footage, pretty clear EVP. I'd be a liar if I said I wasn't excited to have had those results. I keep a very open mind, and what I saw and heard I can't explain: so, what does that leave? To me, it has to be something supernatural. I tend to use 'supernatural' rather than 'paranormal' because that's what these things probably are. A super or powerful natural phenomenon that we don't yet understand."

"And would that include the idea of souls?"

"Ghosts and spirits, you mean?"

"Indeed. The idea that the soul survives and can somehow manifest, or interact with us lot who are left behind?"

Ed began checking camera angles and battery levels. "To me, those kinds of things are all part of nature, as we all are when we're alive. We're all energy. Energy can't be destroyed; it simply changes form. So certainly, I think that's possible – again, part of nature's 'super' side, wouldn't you say?"

"That makes sense to me," Eve replied nodding her head slowly.

"Just a shame I don't come across such phenomena more often."

"Ah, well, you're here now. And believe me, Ed, I know what I've been seeing and hearing. I'm not batty, as I hope you'll agree, and certainly not prone to flights of fancy. I just hope you'll be able to get some evidence – that would be thrilling!"

"I'll do my absolute best for you, Eve," Ed smiled. "I'd be thrilled myself if I captured anything, believe me. It's been a long time."

"Well, I hope Grey Ferns doesn't let you down," Eve laughed.

They set off, and about fifteen minutes later they arrived at the bottom of the east stairs, another grand staircase as befitted the house: spacious first landing, more portraits and wall hangings. As with the rest of the house, all the woodwork was dark oak, encroaching on what little light there was from the chandeliers.

"I'll say goodnight here, Ed."

"I hope you get a good night."

Eve held up her pharmacy bag and rattled it. "I think I will now."

Ed nodded. "Good. Ok, then. See you tomorrow morning." He watched Eve take her first, slow steps, thinking how tired she looked, then moved on to check the rest of the rooms. By the time he returned to the West Wing, it was almost midnight. He dropped himself into the chair, took out a bottle of Pepsi Max and a large box of Pro Plus from the carrier bag and swallowed three of them. Looking at the monitors, everything seemed to be working correctly. He used an A4 notepad to keep initial records, in which he recorded the time, location and description of any event. He made a short note that absolutely nothing had happened in the last thirty minutes then settled back. The first hour was uneventful, so he'd pulled out his book from one of the flight cases and begun to read.

About to glance at his watch, what seemed a moment later, he felt a soft bump on his foot. He looked down, saw his book on the floor, then immediately back at his watch: 02:58am. Damn it. He'd nodded off for almost two hours. He hoped if he'd missed anything that the equipment would have caught it. He'd missed his kip that afternoon, which certainly didn't help. A quick trip to the kitchen to make himself a coffee was probably a good idea.

He got up, took one step –

- and froze.

His brow furrowed. Had he really heard it? A faint but audible thud. Almost immediately it came again. Two in quick succession. He scrutinised the monitors – nothing. Grabbing up a night-vision camcorder, he moved quickly to the next room, and the sound came again, a little louder.

A little closer.

He carried on –

- the next room, nothing –

- then the next, and the next.

Each time nothing looked disturbed, none of the equipment had triggered, and each time the sound got louder.

As he was halfway across the China Boudoir, the thumping became more erratic and almost urgent. It was coming from the east staircase. He slowed down, quieting his footsteps, and crept up to the doorway, keeping tight to the right side. The thud came again, the sound almost on top of him, making his stomach leap. He could already tell it wasn't coming from the foot of the stairs, it was empty, so, very gradually, he brought his head around the doorway, looked up towards the landing – and saw it.

The slippered foot was poking over the top step of the landing, juddering. As he stepped into the hallway, it struck the wall hard several times as if an electric shock had shot through it. And immediately, the penny dropped.

He thundered up the stairs, dropped down beside Eve, who lay on the floor, fitting. Her eyes were fixed in a distant stare, the back of her head bumping up and down off of the carpet, her other limbs jerking. She was in her dressing gown, an empty glass still clutched in her hand.

"Eve! Can you hear me? Eve?" He pulled off his fleece and placed it under her head to stop it hitting the floorboards, and as carefully as he could, slid her hips around, taking her away from the edge of the stairs. He dashed back down, running to the entrance hall which suddenly seemed a long way off. He snatched up the phone, dialled 999, and a minute later, was back on the landing, kneeling at her side.

He took her hand and began talking to her, reassuring her that she'd be ok and that help was on its way.

Although it seemed an eternity, it was only twelve minutes before he saw that wonderful, magnificent hew of blue lights flooding the landing windows. He stood up, watched the ambulance draw up, triggering a sea of luminescence from the security lights, flooding the vast field of rye at the back of the house, and the path that ran alongside it.

And all at once, Ed understood.

FIVE

They'd kept Frank sedated. His head was neatly bandaged, but made it look twice its normal size. A dark purple bruise, edged yellow, covered most of the left side of his face. An odd mix of antiseptic and cooked food pervaded the air, a smell Jon, as a police officer, oddly associated equally with road traffic accidents and new-born babies. He looked on as a nurse checked Frank's drip, thumbed the regulator a little, and updated his record.

The A&E consultant, Philip Mayhew, was on the other side of the bed. "He's had a blood and platelet transfusion and TXA to be on the safe side. With a head wound that deep, sitting there all night with no treatment, I'm astounded he survived. Makes no sense to me at all. He'd lost almost 35% of his volume when he came in, but the wound had stopped bleeding at some point. No clotting at all." He frowned, pulling in his lips. "The bleeding had - well - simply stopped."

"Very odd. Is he out of danger?"

"He's stable, but the results of his head scan are not

good. He hit his head on some kind of skirting board the ambulance crew said, is that right? "

"We think so."

"Well, unfortunately, it fractured his skull. But the nature of the break is extraordinary, something I have never seen before. In a perverse kind of way, he's been extremely lucky. Were you with him at the scene?"

Jon shook his head. One of the island's two ambulances had been parked just before the museum entrance as he'd pulled up in the unmarked car. At the doors had stood Alf Williams, a local trawler-man. On speaking to him, he learned he'd come running up the beach from his boathouse when he'd heard Maureen screaming for help. She'd found the museum unlocked. Going in cautiously, she'd found blood on the floor of the Victorian room, and the skirting of the nursery display. A few moments later she'd tried to get into the kitchen and found the door wouldn't budge. Obviously, she knew something was very wrong, and she'd rushed back out into the street, shouting for help. Alf had managed to barge open the door, to find a pale, unconscious Frank Bernie slumped in a chair in the corner, covered in blood with a dried head-wound. He'd rushed off to call an ambulance, leaving Maureen with Frank. By the time he'd got back from the call box, an ambulance was already there – one advantage to being on a small island.

As Jon thanked Alf for his help and let him go, one of the ambulance paramedics walked up to him.

"Afternoon, Jon."

The police officer nodded. "Afternoon, Ray. How's the patient?"

"In a state of shock, but I think the shoulder is just dislocated rather than broken."

"What about the head wound?"

Ray gave him a sideways look. "Head wound?"

"Alf said he had a head wound."

"Frank did, yes. Maureen slipped on the blood in the kitchen, did her shoulder, but no other injuries. She's in the wagon."

"You're kidding," Jon sighed. "So, where's Frank?"

"He was taken straight to A&E in the first ambulance. No messing around. He didn't look good."

"Do we know how he got his injuries?" Jon had asked.

"From the look of the blood on the floor, we think he probably fell over somehow."

"So why did he barricade himself in the kitchen? Makes me think there might have been others inside the place."

The paramedic had shrugged. "Here," he said dropping a set of keys into Jon's hands. "Maureen asked if you'd lock up once you're finished here."

"Of course. I'll need to pass them on to Jason, our SOCO, though. Thanks for your help, Ray," he said and headed to the main entrance.

Inside he walked carefully through each room, looking hard at everything. He examined the blood in the Victorian room, concluding preliminarily it had none of the hallmarks of an attack, and certainly fitted the idea of a fall as Ray had suggested. But Jason would be able to confirm that, one way or another. As he walked through the museum everything else had looked normal. Nothing disturbed, no damage or signs of forced entry that he could see, which made him wonder again why Frank had blocked the door if no one else had been here.

When he reached the kitchen, it was a different affair: the smashed phone on the floor, the seat in the corner with itself and the surrounding floor covered in dry blood. Yet the worst thing was the smell. It always seemed to be the smell in this job – he'd dealt with just about every kind of situation over the years, involving everything from human excrement, piss, vomit, stale booze, body filth, infected wounds, and worst of all, dead bodies. It was never the sight of anything which he'd found hard to deal with – it was the smell. By the end of the shift it had got into your hair, your uniform, your nose hair and even your eyes, but there was no reason for the kitchen to smell like it had. The blood had dried, and there were no signs of any other bodily fluids. But, he could smell something. Something not right.

He walked around the kitchen a couple of times before he was able to place it – the same odour that had hit him when he'd come home from holiday one hot July to a house that had been without power, and he'd opened his fridge-freezer.

He located the two in the kitchen, and as soon as he had opened them, his head recoiled at the stink. Everything had begun to rot. He moved his hand inside each – it was icy cold. Both were working fine. He frowned, perplexed. He couldn't see how this had anything to do with what had happened: it was just strange - and made the place reek.

Leaving everything else untouched, he'd made his way back out, locked the place up and had driven to A&E. From there, he'd phoned Jason at the nick and arranged for him to examine the scene, telling him to pick the keys up from him at the hospital. He wasn't exactly snowed under. As he'd placed the receiver, Philip Mayhew had approached him and taken him to see Frank in the resus bay.

"Lucky?" Jon did not disguise his doubtful expression, "In what way?"

"A fragment of bone has pierced his primary motor cortex. Every voluntary movement you make is controlled through the PMC. There are very specific regions of this area, controlling a huge variety of body movements – arms, face, fingers and so on. Quite often injuries to the skull like this are messy, and bone fragments shatter. This can cause catastrophic damage to the PMC and cause paralysis in multiple areas of the body. Which is why Frank is so lucky. In his case, we think the single slither of skull has pierced the precise area responsible for leg movement. Quite some force has been applied to the skull – more so than I'd have expected from a simple fall - but it hasn't splintered which is extraordinary. It might sound insensitive, but at least it's only his legs. It's unlikely he'll ever walk again, let alone run, but from the scans, we're hopeful that the rest of his movement will be unaffected. We'll know more when we wake him up this afternoon. It could have been so much worse."

Jon sat down on the chair next to the bed and swept his hands back across his head, "I can understand that, Phil," Jon replied with a resigned tone. "I can, but I'm glad I'm not going to be the one to have to tell him when he wakes up."

SIX

"This is why we must keep our minds clear and balanced and not overthink possible answers, yes? A recent case is an excellent example: a woman in her sixties in a large manor house, reported seeing apparitions, moving furniture and talking pictures in twenty of these rooms. She is also suffering from nausea, dizziness, and fatigue." Dr Dina Melnyk turned a page of her notes and looked up into the darkness of the lecture theatre. "But she was also walking her dog three times a week through rye fields at the rear of the house: and the symptoms of rye ergot poisoning? Nausea, dizziness, fatigue, confusion – sometimes, hallucinations. And unfortunately, in this case, convulsions also." She clicked the switch in her left hand and the slide behind her changed with a quiet whir: a medieval manuscript illustration of a monk.

"Something as simple as a wheat fungus was responsible for a series of so-called 'paranormal' events."

She turned the page of notes slowly, giving time for

the story to sink in. "Remember Ockham's razor that we discussed a few weeks ago?" She glanced up at the slide of English Franciscan monk, William Ockham. "We might have taken this principle from his philosophy, but it can be applied very effectively to our discipline. In a world of fakery and superstition, it becomes invaluable for us. But remember, it does not, as many people think, state that the *simplest* answer is often the correct one." Here, she paused and scanned the lecture theatre, finding focused eyes upon her. "Moreover," she continued, slowing her pace for emphasis, allowing her Ukrainian accent to soften, "it is the explanation that requires the *smallest number of assumptions* that is usually correct. This is right."

She closed her notes on the lectern and smiled. "Thank you, everyone." Much to her surprise, applause began to fill the theatre. Her smile widened, and she nodded her appreciation. "Please have the Dante assignment completed for next week, everyone. Have a good evening."

The projection screen cast milk-blue light across the students as they began packing up, chattering amongst themselves. She began putting away her own things, turning off the lectern lamp, and gathering her books and cue cards together. She spotted her laser pointer sat in the pen well, and as she reached over, knocked her keys to the floor.

"*Layno,*" she cursed, and bent to retrieve them. She checked the heavy but small serrated-steel palm-torch attached to the main keyring, hoping the bulb hadn't broken. It was a very handy thing to have. Her street was not well lit, her driveway obscured by trees at the side making it even worse. It was something she'd been meaning to sort out for a while, but having only moved in three months ago, the task sat at the end of a rather long list. It looked fine, and when she stood up, the young man was standing right in front of the lectern.

She flinched slightly. "Christ, Matthew, what are you wearing, slippers?"

Matthew Stringer was one of the second-year students: an obnoxious, self-important individual, with a very heightened opinion of his academic ability. If he put as much effort into his studies as he did rugby and drinking, he might improve his prospects. Plenty of faculty staff had tried to steer him in the right direction with varying methods, but so far it had all been a waste of time.

She studied him for a second, with his floppy hair, bum-fluff goatee, Gola bag and 'Ace of Base' t-shirt. The sort of person they referred to in her home country as simply '*ledachyy*' - unwilling to work.

"What can I do for you?" she asked as the last of the students filed out of the theatre, leaving just the two of them.

"Wondered if you had any *real* ghost stories, Doctor? You know, stuff you wouldn't teach, but that are really juicy?"

Dina sighed, making no attempt to disguise it. "If I

did, they would be of no value or relevance to the course, Matthew."

"So you have, right?" He moved around the lectern towards her, just a little. "Something we could talk about over a beer, perhaps?" He produced a childish grin.

Dina laughed mildly. "I'm almost old enough to be your mother, am I not?"

The student grinned again. "Yeah, cool."

"Well…" she said, nodding her head slowly, "I do remember one story."

"Awesome. Come on then," he said, slinging his bag over his shoulder, "let's go."

"Wait. It's just a short one. I'll tell it to you now and if you like it, then the drinks are on me."

The youth's eyes widened. "You're on, Doctor."

Dina leaned forward on the lectern. "It happened about a year ago. A woman was returning to her car in a multi-storey. It was Halloween night. The car park was dark and wet with poor lighting, you know what I mean?" The student nodded. "As she reached her car, a figure appeared from the shadows, lunging forward. As it came into the light, she could see the clown costume, Pennywise from 'It'. You know this book?"

Matthew nodded eagerly. "Oh, yeah. One of King's scariest."

"Well, it turned out afterwards that it was just a lazy, self-interested student trying to scare her – a rather sad attempt to get her attention as he'd wanted to ask her out, despite being half her age."

"But what happened when he jumped out at her?"

Dina tucked her notes under her arm, her bag on the other shoulder, and scooped up her keys, letting them dangle in view for a second.

"She broke his jaw in three places with a palm-torch," she said flatly, and watched as his eyes fell on to the keyring and the colour drained from his face. He took a couple of steps back, trying to look casual.

"Ok...cool story...well, I'd better be off, then. Homework and all that. Gotta get that Dante thing done for next week, right?"

Dina nodded very slowly, saying nothing. The student turned and strode off hurriedly towards the rear exit and out into the night, not glancing back even once.

SEVEN

Clara secretly enjoyed the fact that her appearance sometimes intimidated people. In her eyes it simply highlighted their ignorance and conformity to stereotypical judgements. It was the nineties and still so much of society based a person's character and standards on what they wore and the make-up they chose: and it made her rather angry.

However, it wasn't something she had to deal with much at this time of year on the island, as tourists were few, and most of the islanders knew her well, so walking along the seafront now, it was easy to find the headspace she was looking for in the fresh salt air.

She stopped for a moment and looked at her reflection in one of the shop windows: tousled, choppy shoulder length hair, nightshade-black with a deep blue balayage, lipstick colour to match, multicoloured scarf over a short leather jacket, wrists full of bracelets, purple skinny jeans, and white pumps – hardly the look of a serial killer, she thought, chuckling to herself – but enough to shock the occasional old lady and her dog.

She pulled a face at herself, and carried on along the promenade, thinking about the energy fields that had changed so alarmingly over the last few of days. There were plenty of people who dismissed the use of crystals and natural divination, but Clara was no idiot: she knew the science behind it, would have not wasted her time with it if she found none. She had gained a First in her degree a few years ago, her dissertation on the collection methods of scientific evidence in the field of medical near-death experiences getting published in a renowned journal even before her results were through. She had continued with a Masters in the same field, and next year, she planned to do her PhD, examining the range of energy fields associated with 'supernatural' phenomena in human biology and physiology.

When the crystals had begun to react in the way they had, she took it seriously, and it had alarmed her. She had repeated the readings several times a day to observe any inconsistencies, but each time it had been the same – a huge and significant downturn in positive energy.

Her father, despite his initial reservations, hadn't taken long to lend his full support. Spending time with him, showing him examples of her research, and the scientific evidence behind her work, he had, in fact, become very interested in the overall subject. This didn't surprise her : since her mother had cheated on her father with another woman, ten years ago now, they'd grown close. She had inherited Angus's no-nonsense approach to life and people, and rather than this causing a clash, it had enabled them to support each other with more pragmatism than over-sensitivity. They had developed a strong trust in each other, something that particularly helped Angus when it came to running the pub, and Clara when it came to public demonstrations of his confidence and faith in her choice of study subject.

Walking around the island, stepping back a little and observing the daily routine, nothing had seemed out of place, certainly nothing that was obvious. The only thing out of the norm was Frank's accident, but that could easily be just that – an accident, so to attach any significance to that at this stage would be premature - yet without doubt, she could feel a distinctly unpleasant disquiet in the atmosphere. The frustration lay in not knowing why.

The stroll was doing her good though, clearing her head and allowing her to think more logically. Ahead, she saw the sand-powdered stone steps that led from the promenade pavement down on to the beach, so she took them, slipping off her pumps and enjoying the softness beneath her feet. She had to decide what to do. Was it too soon to seek advice? How long should she leave it before she did so? And how bad should she let the readings become before taking action?

She closed her eyes for a moment as she continued along the quiet beach, considering the options, the sound of the waves calming her mind. When she opened them, high up on the park above the sea-front houses, she saw Kyle painting the railings, the sun reflecting of off the fresh paint. She smiled, watching him, thinking herself lucky to be on such a beautiful island, but only briefly, the negativity of the crystals a constant blight on each moment.

One of the ice-cream kiosks was still open and she got herself a ridiculously large cornet, two flakes of course, wandered a little way on up the beach and sat down crossed legged. The tide was some distance off but on its way in, and she watched as she ate, the expanse of shallow, almost flat, criss-cross waves moving in gently, the air tinged with the smell of sunburnt sand.

Maybe she would leave it for a couple of days. If the crystals settled down then she'd need do nothing, but if after that time, the downturn continued, readings of such magnitude just couldn't be ignored.

EIGHT

The library was so calm and reassuring, Brenda Sheraton couldn't possibly have imagined the agony that awaited her. From the moment she entered, her thoughts were firmly focused on nothing else but the task at hand, keeping at bay her own nightmare that she was having to deal with.

Though small, it was thoroughly and eclectically stocked. Beautifully appointed, it was evident from the neat posters, information boards and themed wall decorations that her sister had a deep passion for helping the islanders have access to as much help as was available in terms of the community: something she had never realised until now.

She passed behind the front desk and went into the cosy office beyond. She placed her suitcase and floral canvass travel-bag gently against the back wall. She then removed her tired raffia bow hat and neatly plucked her faux leather gloves from each finger, placing them inside it. Taking off her long, wool tweed coat (a wonderful bargain from the Scope shop back in

February), she placed all three neatly on top of the luggage. She turned, clamping her hands together excitedly, and decided to make herself a nice cup of tea.

A few minutes later she was sipping hot Tetley's, listening to the muffled steps of people moving from shelf to shelf, along with the occasional flutter of book pages. Some of the most peaceful sounds she'd heard in a long time.

She was so excited about looking after the library for the afternoon. Her sister, Audrey, was the chief librarian - by virtue of the fact she was the only librarian, which tickled Brenda. Audrey had asked her to step in whilst she attended a hospital appointment. It was the kind of arrangement that Brenda found so charming and was so typical of this lovely little island: being asked to take on such a task as nonchalantly as if she'd been asked to pop next door and ensure her neighbours rice pan didn't boil over.

She loved the fact that the island had everything it needed – hospital, school, volunteer fire service, good bus service and even a small cinema. Everything essential to the islanders. With the parade of tourist boutiques, cafés, and typical town shops on the 'Borrow', was it? – and everyone popping home to the Lend (she knew that one) at the end of the working day, she thought more regular stopovers with her sister from now on would be a marvellous idea. The dreadful silence that greeted her when she awoke each morning, and whenever she arrived home from anywhere, was already unbearable. Spending more time with Audrey would be most comforting.

So, the opportunity to chat with people, help them with their book borrowing and so on was going to be so enjoyable. It was a pity she could not stay on the island longer, but she had to be at the airport by 1pm tomorrow – ferry to the mainland at 7am, then a five-hour coach trip to London, so it would be an early night as well. Maybe a couple of sherries and a natter with Audrey after dinner, but that would have to be it.

If all went well, Richard would arrive back from Australia within the next five days. She'd booked herself into a modest B&B, and had organised his collection from Heathrow with a local funeral director, who would then transport him home. She insisted on handing in the original paperwork and making the payment in person, unable to bear the idea of something going wrong, and Richard being left over there, all alone.

Brenda had always been very untrusting when it came to financial matters. As a young woman, she'd never even opened a bank account. Her wages had been paid in cash for much of her early working life, and when progress forced her salary to reach her by BACS, the day it went in, she withdrew every penny and transferred it to a large cash tin she kept in the airing cupboard. Richard had allowed her to do the same with his money. Typical of him – anything to keep her happy, nothing ever too much trouble and so laid back. There seemed to be very little in life that ever bothered him.

Taking another long sip of tea, she wondered how she'd manage now. Richard's life insurance had not covered the repatriation costs, and she'd had to use up all of her savings to cover the shortfall. Worth every penny of course, but it still left her worried about how she was going to cope on just her pension, and half of Richard's. Thankfully they had moved into council assisted housing a couple of years ago, so at least that was sorted.

She drew her lips in and sighed. As long as she could pay her bills and eat, that was all that mattered, wasn't it? That was the best way to view it. "Stiff upper lip, old girl," as Richard would have told her. "Worse things happen in my garden shed," he would say, always making her laugh.

Quite suddenly, she turned, put down her mug and went straight to her travel-bag. She threw open the zip, slid her hand down the near side and was reassured the moment her fingertips touched the money. Checking that all four large, neatly wrapped bundles were still there next to the paperwork, she zipped it back up, shoulders relaxing.

After a last moment in thought, she left the office and came into the clear, soft light that filled the library. She sat in the rather modern looking wheelie chair behind the desk, a big blue angle-poise lamp helping her read the list of instructions Audrey had left. All very straight forward. She was particularly looking forward to using the 'bleeper' as her sister described it: the scanner that recorded books in and out. According to the instructions (and several recent telephone coaching sessions with Audrey), all she had to do was point the fat end at the bar code on each book, whether it was going out or coming in, and the computer did the rest. As long as it 'bleeped', then all was fine. If it didn't, then the customer either couldn't take the book out, or if they were returning it, just had to hang on to it. Her sister would sort any such issues out on her return.

She looked at the PC monitor sat directly in front of her. A bulbous version of herself reflected back: mousey-grey back-combed hair, ruddy cheeks, and a delicate mouth. She only ever used the tiniest amount of makeup, just to give her some colour, and kept her appearance neat and simple. At sixty-two, she was still proud of her figure, having managed to keep it at a size 14 (or 16 depending upon the manufacturer, which annoyed her somewhat). Since losing Richard however, the weight had begun to fall off her, something she was aware of, yet at the moment, could do little about. She simply had no appetite, though Audrey assured her it would return in time.

The screen was full of colourful shapes, each filled with letters or numbers, and the 'bleeper' sat on the desk to her right. She patted it a couple of times, as if reassuring a nervous lapdog. Ok, she was all set.

The afternoon passed very pleasantly. She enjoyed the brief, but interesting, conversations with borrowers, all done in hushed tones as if they each were trusting each other with some kind of secret. A toddler group came in for a while to have stories read to them by their teacher in the children's corner while older students drifted in and out, and the steady stream of elderly customers – those over eighty as far as Brenda was concerned – rarely waned. A quirk she found especially quaint was the subdued sound of the seashore that crept in each time someone entered the library. It lifted her spirits. Losing Richard so suddenly and unexpectedly had wrenched her world apart. The barrage of continuous thoughts and emotions were almost too much to bear at times, but her certain, unshakeable belief that she'd be reunited with him again one day was what kept her going. She knew it beyond any doubt. And it never failed to comfort her whenever she thought the grief would consume her very being. Hanging on to that conviction kept her alive – some days, she felt like she was just existing – but knowing she would hold him again one day, would always bring her back to life. Brenda was a proud woman, and there was never any question of letting such emotion show: any stranger would be forgiven for thinking her world was fine and rosy.

Although she had not carried on her catholic upbringing into adult life, she had taken away from it a strong belief in the afterlife. The soul carried on, the body just a physical vessel for its time on earth – an infinitesimal part of its endless journey. Two of her friends had had personal experiences of such a nature, further strengthening her credence, and for Brenda now, it was a simple certainty.

Around four o'clock, visitors began to thin out, so she'd started tidying shelves and tables. She loved the way her feet hardly made a noise on the thick carpet as she moved about. Each time she did something, gathered up a pile of newspapers, slid books away or tucked a chair in, the sound was all but swallowed by the stillness of the room.

The bookshelves that filled most of the room were almost ceiling height and stretched far back. Brenda knew how much her sister wanted to have a range of books that would appeal to as wide a cross-section of the community as possible, and as such, had sacrificed her private desk and office space to allow for more shelving. The only problem was it made putting back books rather awkward as the space between each shelf was rather narrow. However, the generous lighting, pale pine woodwork and cream carpets offset any feelings of restriction it might otherwise have brought about.

When she finally returned to her wheelie-chair, a feature of the library that was fast becoming her favourite – (it was so comfortable on her lower back) – she glanced up at the clock. It was almost five. An hour to go before closing time. There was just one visitor left: she remembered seeing them very briefly in shadow at the opposite end of a shelf she'd been returning books to, finger tracing along titles, obviously looking for something specific. She decided not to offer any help as she knew nothing about the library - other than the 'bleeper' and how to make a cup of tea. What a good idea, she thought – another cuppa. She reached for her mug, and as her hand took the handle, she heard the sudden and unmistakable rattling of spoons against china from behind her.

She let out an involuntary "Oh!", turned in her chair and looked into the office. Through the open door, she could see her luggage against the back wall. To the left, were the two kitchen units on which the kettle sat, along with a cluster of tea mugs and a fan of spoon handles protruding from one of them. She raised her eyebrows, wondered for a second if grief could make you hear things - that thought immediately vanishing as the spoon handles began jouncing off the inside of the mug, trembling and striking against each other like fresh fish in an empty bucket.

Brenda frankly didn't believe what she was seeing. It was the stress she was under. That was it. She may be putting on that brave face, but the reality was, she was crumbling under the weight of her sorrow.

She blinked rapidly and, pinching her nose with her forefinger and thumb, closed her eyes for a second. The noise stopped and when she looked back, the spoons were still.

Of course they were.

Then a new noise grabbed her attention – the sound of soft footsteps – and she remembered the last visitor left in the library. She felt a small flush of relief. A little light conversation would bring her back to her senses – yes, that would do it. That would be a nice way to end the day.

She got up, and left the desk. There was a notable sunless tone to the library now, as if someone had covered every bulb in a thin layer of ash. She wondered if the lights went on to some kind of power-saving mode when it got near to closing time. Suddenly an environment that had felt so clement and benign became so sullied by a simple change in lighting, sending a small shiver down her spine.

Of course, it was all in her imagination - she knew that. Now where had that visitor got to?

She took a general look, up and down the room, couldn't see anyone anywhere, so went over to the left side of the shelves to begin her search. The adjacent wall displayed community posters: help for carers, support for mental health, 'new parent' coffee mornings and one she'd particularly noticed earlier on: two older couples sat around a garden table, all laughing together, having a wonderful time by all appearances. It was something to do with equity release, but it was the faces of the people that held her attention: they cut so deep. None of them in that photo having to deal with the loss of their partner. They still had them. They could still hold them and hug and kiss them goodnight.

The two women were sat at the table, the bald man behind one of them with his hands on her shoulders, and the other man – grey hair, but with those lighter temples where once he'd been blonde.

Just like Richard.

Smooth brow, faded freckles, jowls beginning to wrinkle – but not *just* like Richard.

She stopped.

Stared.

Squinted, focusing in the pallid light.

It *was* Richard

And as she watched the man in the poster tilted his head fully towards her, the movement as if he were on time-lapse, his smile widening, she could see for certain.

Tears clouded her eyes instantly and her hands flew to her mouth.

His head stopped turning, and jerkily, his hand came up from his side, reaching out towards her, beckoning.

Brenda moved closer. "Richard! Oh my lord. My dear Richard."

She reached out towards his hand –

- and screamed as his face contorted into a twisted rage, his teeth bared, his eyes entirely black, and all but his middle finger curling down into his tight fist.

She recoiled, screaming again. The sound filled equally with repulsion and despair, tears pouring down her cheeks, and involuntarily she slammed her hands up against the poster, covering the hideous face. She held them there for several seconds, before letting them slide away. She knew what she'd see: just an ordinary poster, with two older couples sat around a garden table, all laughing together…

… having a wonderful time…

…by all appearances.

And she was right.

She slumped back against the shelf behind her, forcing her sobs to slow, her hands visibly quivering. How long would this last? How long would it take her to cope with such loss? The pain would never go, but surely there must come a time when she would be able to deal with life again?

She suddenly wondered if the visitor had seen any of her hysterics? She looked tentatively left and right. Thankfully, no one was there.

She took another few minutes to calm herself down, allowing thoughts of a friendly, reassuring chat with the visitor to fill her mind. She heard the soft footfalls again. They were nearby; at least that would save her searching the entire library, something she certainly did not want to do after such an episode. Show them out, get back to the desk and the wheelie chair and wait for Audrey. That was now the plan.

Carrying on towards the end of the shelf, she turned, expecting to find the stranger there, but no. They must be near the next couple of shelves along, as again, she heard another carpeted step.

The height of the shelves stole an unhealthy share of the light from the room as Brenda moved between the first two, eyes scanning over the top of the books to see if she could catch sight of her last patron. She reached the end, turned –

- and heard the clatter of spoons jarring against china.

But she didn't. Not really.

She knew that.

She couldn't help but look towards the office as she stepped out from the end of the shelves. She scolded herself, turned towards the next row-

- and saw him.

Richard.

Standing half behind the very end shelf, half out. Despite the room's illumination, deep shadow seemed to blunt his features, shadow that didn't make sense under such lighting. But what Brenda could see of those features, and more the silhouette, she knew it to be Richard.

"Brenda," he said, the movement of his mouth distorted by the tenebrosity. But his voice was firm and confident – as it always was.

She couldn't reply.

"You knew you would see me again." He said.

She thought maybe, in the shadows, she saw him smile gently.

"But not this soon, eh, old girl?" She loved it when he called her that: a habit that had stayed with him all their years together. He offered a hand.

"Come on. Come and see me. Be with me again."

Once again, tears welled, and the rush of overpowering love was too much for her to control, regardless of what she knew her mind was doing to her.

She started forward as he offered out both hands.

A few steps more with her heart racing, the indescribable joy of having her dear Richard before her once again, almost too much.

She raised her arms and put her hands out towards him.

Another step –

- and she reached him as his face contorted into a twisted rage, his teeth bared, his eyes entirely black. The exact same vision of malignance she'd seen in the poster. Impulsively, she recoiled, almost falling and grabbed the corner of a shelf to save herself.

But '*It*' came no further.

Not Richard.

'*It*'.

It stood still; its face still set in that grotesque form. But its voice was still Richard's, calm and soothing.

"You'll never see me again, dear Brenda. I'm gone. I'm nothing. My consciousness died with my body. Forget all that life-long bullshit you believe in, my flesh is rotting in a zinc box in the bowels of an aircraft, old girl."

"No!" Brenda screamed. "You're not him, you're not my Richard."

"Then why am I here? I've been given the chance to tell you the truth, old girl." He laughed quietly – "to stamp out your childish expectations."

"It's not true. I *will* see him again. I know it." She began backing up, heard the spoons dancing again in the office.

It shook its head slowly.

"You will die alone, old girl, as I, your husband, did. You'll die knowing for certain that nothing awaits you at all. Just oblivion. Knowing that you'll never, ever see me again." It began slowly moving forward again, and she continued to back up, hands out behind her, trying to guide herself toward the desk, to the wheelie-chair, and the safe circle of light from the big blue angle-poise.

"You will never touch me again. Never feel my breath on your cheek. Never hear me call you 'old girl'."

She felt the edge of the wall, knowing the door frame was next, and opposite that, the desk.

"Never, *ever* again."

It carried on towards her, still slowly. But she felt the doorframe, turned, and ran as well as she could towards the desk, the fact only dawning on her as she reached it that through the office doorway she was watching the spoons dance frenziedly in the mug –

- and the kettle beginning to spin, vapour blasting from its spout as the water boiled furiously without stopping, its loose plug thrashing around at the end of its wire. The lights began to spark, streaks of electricity arcing between them and all the plug points. The taps were full-on, scolding water thundering into the small sink, gushing from the cupboard underneath as pipes burst and ripped open.

And then –

- electricity hit water.

There was a deafening hiss, followed by what sounded like rapid gunfire as flames erupted from every socket in the room.

Brenda cried out, hands shooting forward in a futile gesture as, within a second, flames licked at her luggage and began feeding on it. She rushed for the office, and at once the wheelie chair careered across the room, slamming sharply into her back.

She hit the floor hard, but her desperation drove her on.

She pulled herself up, grimacing as the pain lanced along her spine. She took three more steps –

- and the PC monitor flew from the desk, the edge slicing into her left leg: she heard a moist 'snap', and collapsed to her knees with a scream. Looking up, she saw the flames engulf her hat and coat, moving swiftly down them and on to her travel-bag.

She cried out in both pain and despair, but despite the agony, she didn't stop. The pain didn't matter. It was irrelevant. She began crawling, pulling at the floor in front of her with her fingernails, reaching the doorway, the carpet giving her just a little more purchase. The smell of smoke was now thick in her nostrils as it began to fill the office. She continued to crawl, her left foot pushing hard against the floor, her right failing to respond, flailing from side to side like a broken mop.

But it just didn't matter to her.

Richard mattered to her.

Richard was all that had ever mattered to her.

As she managed to drag herself through the doorway, she looked up and saw her travel-bag just a few feet away, eager flames curling all around its edges. She was near enough now for the heat to start stinging her skin.

But it was just a few more feet.

Just a few more feet, Brenda.

Just keep going, her mind screamed at her.

She hauled herself forward with a shriek of pain, reached out with one hand, stretching, fingers grasping – and heard the scrape of metal on melamine, the kettle flying from the side, smashing into the side of her skull and she crumpled to the floor, a broken moan escaping her lips as the edge of her vision began to cloud. If she could have screamed anymore, she would have, as she watched the flames envelope her entire travel-bag through her misted eyes.

"Richard…" she mouthed silently, her sight fading completely, as did everything around her.

NINE

The figure sat cross-legged in front of the large headstone, cradling the book, bound in black leather, pages fragile with age – and looked about cautiously. The hooded top helped anonymity, and the other headstones clustered close around would make it difficult to be spotted: and besides, the likelihood of anyone being up here on the sand-shelf was highly unlikely. The decrepit cemetery was surrounded by woodland, rough thicket weaving in and out of the graves that led to the edge of the shelf.

Here, the figure could carry out whatever experiment they wanted to, test any incantation, try out anything from the old texts without the slightest risk of discovery. There was a good line of sight to the beach when kneeling up, if required, and the only path through the thicket to the beach was a good fifty feet away – a path that looked seldom trod, probably known to very few people, if any on the island. All angles were covered.

The figure took out two black candles from a rucksack, pushed them into the hard sand either side of the headstone and lit them. With a piece of chalk from a pocket, the figure began marking the headstone, carefully following the instructions in the book, keeping as close to the illustrations as possible.

Maybe this would work. The figure hoped to God it would.

Finishing the first pattern on the gravestone, the sound of rustling thicket made the figure freeze. It began to get louder, coming from the direction of the small path. And a moment later, the figure saw the old man emerge from the last of the wooded area, thrashing at the undergrowth with a stick, some kind of bag on his back.

The figure ducked down, close up against the headstone, and listened. And only when the sound of the stick and footsteps had completely disappeared, did the figure dare raise its head. After looking carefully around, it was clear no one else was about. But the old man had spooked the figure – that was enough – it was too risky now. What if he came back in the middle of the incantation? It was no good.

Angrily, the figure blew out the candles, shoved everything back into the rucksack, checked around once more, and moved off through the cemetery towards the woods.

TEN

It was just after 6pm when he had seen her, even though no-one had believed him. He remembered that after looking at the new watch his father had bought him for his birthday three days ago.

She had been standing on the far bank of the river that ran through the grounds of the estate, and he had watched her for some thirty seconds or so. At first, he had not been sure. The misty rain that had continued since early dawn had blurred her features and the gusting wind tugging at the pink rhododendrons next to her, obscuring the view every few seconds.

Even so, he had not taken his eyes off of her and the more he had stared, the clearer she had seemed to become. From his third floor bedroom window in the huge house, he was looking down on her, and when, finally, she'd looked up at him, slowly raised a hand to her lips, and blew him a kiss, there was no doubt – it was his mother.

At that moment, he had rushed down six flights of stairs, shoes clattering on the uncarpeted oak and into the grand dining room where his father was holding the party.

The room was filled with cigarette smoke, music, flashing lights, and the sound of laughter. He could see his father towards the back of the room, dancing with his aunty, wine glass in hand. Pushing through the rest of the gyrating adults who, either patted him on the head, or groped at his hands to try and get him to dance, he reached his father out of breath and almost shaking.

He'd tugged at his trouser leg and his father had taken him into the billiard room next door, knelt down and asked him what the matter was. When he told him he'd seen his mother standing on the riverbank, his father had been kind, but firm. He told him that mother was in Cairo and not to worry as she'd be back in a few days.

He insisted he had seen her, over and over. His father had been patient and, in the end, took his hand, and told him to show him where he had seen her.

Taking his father out through the front of the great house, he had guided him around to the right of the building, into the ornamental gardens and pointed across the riverbank and the space next to the rhododendrons –

- which was empty.

His father had put it down to the fact that he missing his mother and his overactive imagination, and at first, he had argued, quite vehemently. His father had remained kind, and when it became obvious that, despite this, he was never going to believe him, he gave up.

They walked back to the house, talking about how much they were both looking forward to her return, and leaving his father at the door to the dining hall, he'd gone to the library and sat on one of the great bay-window seats overlooking the farm fields that rolled out to the horizon itself, book in hand.

He had eventually fallen asleep, his father coming in and waking him at around 11pm. He had shaken him gently and with tears in his eyes, told him of his mother's death. At around 8pm she had been on her way to a business meeting at a restaurant in the centre of town, and had been struck by a stolen car feeling from the police.

The following days had been a blur of tears, so it was some time before he had come to realise, with everyone around him constantly talking about it all, that Cairo was two hours ahead –

- and that the moment Ed had seen his mother blow him a kiss, she had already gone.

ELEVEN

Jon expected his SOCO to laugh when he mentioned it, but he sat there, a large chip disappearing into his mouth, and just looked at him.

"Ghosts, Jason. Flying nannies? Oh, please. When I took his statement he'd not been awake that long. I think the man was still out of it."

Jason swallowed and pushed his lunch to one side. They sat at one of the many picnic tables that ran along the wide promenade. The main road behind them followed the seafront and before his SOCO had arrived, Jon had nipped across to the esplanade opposite to grab some fish and chips for lunch.

"I'm not saying I believe any of that, I'm just saying the whole place was bloody odd."

Jon regarded his SOCO. Jason was thoroughly reliable, even for a civvy, and took his work seriously. A tall, wiry young man in his early thirties, he always looked as if he'd just got out of bed: glasses perched on the end of his nose, creased uniform and shoes that belonged in a landfill. But his attention to his work bordered on OCD and his eye for detail was of a level Jon had rarely seen before. He'd come over to the island from the distant universe of the HQ when Jon had been promoted to sergeant, and he'd warned him that other than the occasional burglary, or theft from a motor vehicle, he'd be engaged in a lot of thumb-twiddling. Even so, every job the man did, he did with the care and attention as if it were the crime of the century. So respect for Jason was something Jon certainly did not lack.

"Odd in what way?"

"Maybe you should take Frank's statement again when he's back home?"

"Thanks for that, Sherlock. In what way?"

Jason reached into a large black bag that sat at his side and pulled out his report.

"Ok, so, Frank saying he fell after his 'scare', shall we call it, is consistent with the blood patterns, and the shape of his wound matches that of the skirting at the bottom of the nursery display." He ran a finger down the page a little.

"And the blood trail to the kitchen, and in there, is all Frank's. I couldn't find any prints other than his, Maureen's and the cook's. And I spent some considerable time looking."

Jon finished his last mouthful of chips, nodding. The smell of vinegar and sea air belied the soberness of the meeting. The sky was blue again, but the offshore breeze cut a chill. "Ok. Well it looks like we can rule out foul play at the moment then."

"Agreed."

"Anything else conclusive?"

"Nope. Everything ties up with Frank's version of events."

"Except the flying nanny," Jon said, his mouth shifting to one side.

"So, on to the weird stuff." The SOCO flipped a page. "As far I can tell, none of this is actually related to the incident, so unless you tell me otherwise, I'll be keeping it out of the final report, ok?"

"My thoughts exactly."

"As usual, I took photos from the start of the scene through to the end. The first bizarre find was the wall plaster I found around the nursery display. At first, I thought they might be from someone throwing punches, but the stuff was just falling away from the wall. When I tried taking samples, it just came away in clumps. It was damp, and I mean, dangerously damp. In a building constructed in that way, 'wall-collapsingly' dangerous. I examined the plaster on some more panels – same again, coming off in lumps – like clay." The SOCO paused, opening the can of Pepsi Jon had bought him. He took a quick mouthful and carried on, noticing Jon looking relatively unmoved.

"The second weird thing was the kitchen."

"The smell, right?" Jon asked. "I got a lung full of that when I first went in."

"Yeah, but not just that. The rust."

Jon frowned. "Rust?"

"I'm telling you, Jon, it was like walking into the wreck of the Titanic. Every inch of metal in that room was caked in half an inch of hardened rust at the edges. Utterly nuts."

"The place looked normal when I went in. What was that, about, an hour before you?"

Jason nodded and checked his report. "Yeah, pretty much."

"And you're sure it was just rust?"

Jason pulled a face. "You don't think I know what rust is?"

"Sorry, stupid question. I agree, that's strange."

"Like I keep saying. Then it was the stink. You know what that was?" Jon told him about the rotting food.

"Exactly, and as you said, both of those appliances work perfectly. Again, utterly nuts."

"Can I ask, is 'utterly nuts' a technical term?" Jason gave him a deadpan look. Jon held up his hands apologetically. "Carry on."

"After my main examination, I left the kitchen and started to take a look at any more metal work I could find. It wasn't much. As you know the place is an old wool house, all plaster, and beams with the odd door handles, hinges and so on." He turned another page, looked up at Jon. "All covered in rust. Not as thick as in the kitchen, but getting there. And if you think that's weird, there was also the mould." He took another sip from the can.

"Going back into the entrance hall via the various rooms, I started to notice it in the corners of the display cases. Every single one."

"Something that was already there, surely?" Jon said.

"Let me finish. Finally, there was the dry rot. Know anything about that?" Jon shook his head. "It's a fungus that thrives in humid conditions in wood, and basically starts to eat it. Again, damp, is the main cause, same with mould."

Jon looked doubtful. "Come on, Jason, you just told me how old that place is. That could have been there for years, and you just noticed it because of the other stuff you were finding."

"But listen to this. I know what dry rot is but I'm certainly no expert. So I stopped and spoke to Kyle on the way back to the nick. He's repainting the top park railings at the moment. I showed him the pics I'd taken and he reckoned, for the rot to get that bad, it had to have been there for six or seven years."

"Like I said, it's old."

"Kyle told me that he'd help fit new beams in that place six months ago. About half of them were replaced." The SOCO closed his report, drained his can. "At least eight of the new ones had the dry rot, explain that to me."

Jon raised his eyebrows. "Bizarre."

"Utterly nuts."

"Do you reckon any of this at all has anything to do with the incident? I agree with you, now, it's very strange, but I can't see how any of it changes the evidence we have about what happened."

Jason slipped the report into his bag and pulled out a ring binder. "Absolutely none of it as far as I can tell." He opened the folder, taking out a plastic sleeve. "But here's the best bit," he said, taking a few photographs from it. He laid some in a row on the table. "Here are the shots of the place when I went in. Look at the display cases. Look at the door handles."

Jon peered at them, bringing his head forward. The display cases were clear, and the door handles reflected some of the flash. Jason then produced the same number of photos, of the same subjects, and laid them exactly below the first row.

"Now look at these." Brown, flaking rust had started to creep around the edges of the door handles and around the corners of the display cases, the appearance of deep blue mould was clear to see.

The police officer looked at Jason with a bewildered expression.

"I took the bottom row an hour after the top, Jon." The SOCO gathered up the photos, returned them to his bag.

He stood up.

"Just one hour."

TWELVE

The old cemetery was one of the strangest places on the island. It was also one of Ernest Gibson's favourites, which he'd have thought unspeakably ironic if he'd known what lay ahead.

Dating back to the early 1100s, when a church used to stand several hundred feet inland from the edge of it, the archaic graves went almost to the edge of the sand-ridge and most were now overgrown by waist-high thicket. Below, less than fifteen feet, was the beach. Wide and sweeping, always with high waves, and much loved by young surfers.

The OAP always used the path that led through the cemetery. It kept him away from prying eyes. In all the years he'd been using the overgrown path through the thicket, he'd never met another soul, which usually allowed him to reach the beach unnoticed. He was younger than his appearance suggested – very much by design, rather than by accident. He kept his thinning hair greasy, his nails filthy, and shaved maybe twice a week. Most of his clothes saw the inside of a washing machine once a month, as he found the smell particularly effective in keeping up his 'senile old fool' masquerade.

Being seen as some decrepit old octogenarian went a long way to deflecting suspicion that he was capable of committing any kind of crime nowadays, let alone kiddie fiddling. They had never been able to get anything on him – not a morsel. Never would. He was far too clever to allow that to happen with years of experience teaching him how to cover his tracks exceptionally well. As he used his stick (which he didn't need) to beat energetically at the few parts of the undergrowth that hindered him as he made his way through the leaning and broken gravestones, he smirked to himself, enjoying the strength he still had at seventy-one.

Slung over one shoulder, was his light-weight camping chair, folded into its carrying bag, along with a small, packed lunch. Around his neck lay his pride and joy: a Casio QV-10. One of the first decent digital cameras to land on the market. It had a massive 2MB memory and could hold up to a staggering, ninety-six high-resolution photos. But best of all was that the lens swivelled so he pointed it at whoever he wanted but gave the impression he was photographing something completely different. He'd put a brand-new memory card in before setting out, to ensure it didn't fill up too quickly and cause him to miss out on any particularly good shots.

The salt air began to mingle with the aroma of the

sand-and-earth mix beneath his feet, a smell unique to this journey through the ancient boneyard, setting butterflies flitting in his gut. Moments later, he reached the edge of the sand-shelf, gravestones still pushing up to the end.

He turned and stepped carefully along the ridge, soon coming to the gentle slope that led to the beach and made his way down. Setting his chair up near to the bottom of the sand-shelf (it kept the sea breeze off of his neck), he put his lunch box on his lap and checked his camera settings.

A few young surfers were already there, but today, he'd hit the bonus. Someone had obviously brought along their little sister. She was sat a bit further up the beach in the shallows, using her hands to continually splash water across her legs. The surfers wouldn't usually pack up until late afternoon, so he had plenty of time. He shuffled down into the chair, crossed his legs, and clasped his hands across his chest, sighing contentedly. He'd enjoy the view for a while before putting his QV-10 into use.

The wind was still way offshore, kicking up rollers, so he was quite warm in his long, shabby coat, woolly hat and tattered fleece trousers. He turned his head and glanced at the sand-shelf. It was something he did every time he came here, couldn't help it – wondering how close and how far down the remains of coffins were: if there was even anything left now. Always unnerving to think they might only be a few feet back from his head, but as always, he dismissed the ridiculous thought.

It was always a relief to get out of the house. The walls seemed to close in as autumn did the same, the thickset leylandii, both front and back, hindering much of the sunlight throughout the year for most of each day. He didn't have the money to get them removed, and keeping lights on all damn day was way too expensive. By late morning he felt as if it were hard to catch his breath and a constricting panic would crawl into his stomach and begin gnawing away at him the longer he stayed inside. Tunnels, tube stations, revolving doors, lifts – all such places triggered his claustrophobia. So, The Black Dog had become a regular bolt hole, or long walks in the park near the lower school, weather permitting. The foot of the sand-shelf was always his first choice, but soon it would be too cold for that as well.

He opened the Tupperware box on his lap and took out a sandwich: fish paste. As he pushed half of it into his mouth as if he hadn't eaten for a week, his mind wandered back to how the phobia had all begun. He was fourteen, an adventure weekend with his Boys Brigade company: the 15th Willard. He was working towards his first rank of Lance Corporal, and had gained some important recognition on the Saturday: abseiling, canoeing, raft building, and leadership games: but then, Sunday had brought with it the potholing.

At first, it had been ok. The entrance to the cave system had been wide and high, but quite suddenly, a hundred feet in, everyone had to switch on their headlamps as the darkness became absolute and the cave quickly became a tight gnarled tube of solid rock. They'd been told to turn off their headlamps and he was immediately blind. Even with his hand almost touching his face, it was completely invisible, sending a bolt of uncontaminated panic through his whole body. He was desperate not to look like a sissy and certainly not do anything to risk his chances of promotion, so he had taken a deep breath and waited for the instruction to turn the helmet lights back on.

Water dripped continually from the crevices, making the rock slippery, a faintly acrid smell all around. He was in the middle of the line, the smaller boys at the front with an instructor and brigade leader, and the taller boys to the rear, another brigade leader ensuring no one got left too far behind.

For a while, the going was pretty easy. Until the pothole began to incline upwards. The damp rock made it extremely difficult to get any footing, the hole becoming even smaller as he ascended. He could feel the panic rising in him again, a terrifying, neanderthal reaction as thoughts began to rush through his mind -

- how many hundreds of feet of solid rock were above him?

- being hemmed in by the boys around him, unable to get past them -

- unable to even turn around -

- or how it would be impossible to be rescued?

- how long would the air last?

His arms were becoming restricted as the hole tightened, and he began to struggle to move them up his sides and in front to find a new grip. When he arrived at the top, he burst into tears, acute fear erupting inside again as he saw the hole he now had to crawl through. He had no way of stopping himself, regardless of how embarrassed he felt. He could see the smaller boys and the brigade leader on the other side of the hole and could see that the cave opened up again considerably.

The instructor had perched himself on a small ledge to the side of the aperture. Ernest had frozen, his mind turning every muscle to stone. He began screaming, a hammock of snot swinging from nose to cheek as he shook his head, refusing to listen to the instructor as the man constantly reassured him he could fit through. When the man, (who was well-muscled and at least six foot) explained that if he was able to fit through, so was Ernest, the penny finally dropped.

It did nothing to assuage the raw fear inside, the sense of complete helplessness, the loss of control, but it did get him through the hole. It was another twenty minutes before they came back up through a forty-five-degree exit tunnel and he remembered kissing the ground, running his hands through the grass, vowing silently never again to venture beneath it.

A fresh gust of wind from offshore brought him back to the beach, and he refocused his gaze, allowing it, once again, to land on the girl, who was now digging holes with her feet in the wet sand.

He crammed the remaining half of the sandwich into his mouth, and, once he'd finished, leant his head back on the chair and shut his eyes, listening to the gulls. Soon he began to dose lightly, only half aware of his surroundings. Which was why at first, he took no notice of the sound, but when it came again, it perforated his slumber and he sat up with a start, his lunch box falling from his lap.

Scratching. Like fingernails on wood. Audible, but still faint enough that it was impossible to tell where it came from.

Very peculiar.

He laid his head back down, and as it touched the chair the scratching came again. This time it was louder. He peered at the sand around him – maybe it was a gull fiddling with some old ice-cream wrapper. But there was nothing to see.

Then, just for a fleeting moment, he swore he could smell that acrid odour from the pothole invading his nose, that identical panic from fifty-seven years ago threatening to rear up again.

But no, sea air filled his nostrils.

It was his imagination.

Of course it was.

Then again, came the scratching. This time, not just a single sound, as if whatever were making it, there were more of them. Grating, scraping at something. A slither of unease sidled into his chest, and his breath started to become shallow. This was not right. Maybe old age was finally creeping up on him and he was beginning to hear things? Whatever was happening, he didn't like it.

Taking hold of the sides of the chair, he shuffled it backwards, hard up against the sand-shelf, hoping to feel more secure. He pulled his coat around himself, tucked his feet under the chair, and waited for the sound again. If he heard it one more time, he was off.

Gulls continued to screech above.

End waves broke gently on the shore.

He even heard a ship's horn far off in the distance.

But no more scratching.

He relaxed a little, his shoulders dropping, letting his coat fall open.

As he ran his fingers over his head in a gesture of relief, the wet, putrid hands grabbed his wrists, more sliding around his face, clamping over his mouth, stifling his scream.

More arms burst from the sand-shelf behind him, decomposed muscle over blackened bone, grabbing his hair, his neck, clamping down on his shoulders, pushing him violently forward so more hands could wrap around his chest. The stench of diseased meat filled his mouth and nose from the hands across his face and he gagged but as he did so, the grip around his chest tightened, and acute desperation to breathe   fused with the terror already coursing through him.

Then, in one powerful movement, he was wrenched from his chair, backwards, upside down and headfirst through the wall of the sand-shelf. Sand filled his eyes, nose and ears as the hands continued to drag him further in. His breathing reflex kicked in and he could do nothing to prevent his mouth opening and immediately packing with sand. In all this claustrophobic nightmare, he could feel his legs still dangling outside from the knees down, and in some kind of desperate attempt to attract attention, began thrashing them around.

But this pathetic action lasted less than a few seconds. He began to suffocate, the pain crushing his lungs, his mind convulsing in abject horror. Unconsciousness began sliding over him as the hands dragged him further in, until nothing was left to see but his feet poking out of the sand-shelf.

Then, all at once, there was silence.

And if a stranger had happened to be standing in the thicket above, if they listened very carefully, they may just about have heard the clicking of a digital camera beneath their feet –

- again

- and again

- and again.

THIRTEEN

Angus had shut the pub early. Dusk had brought with it ferocious squalls, rain so hard it rattled the window latches. He'd pulled a low table and the two largest sofas in front of the fire, and lit it. The flames painted dense, flickering shadows across the walls, and brass ornaments, rows of glasses bouncing back the light in amber hues. By the time everyone had turned up, it was a roaring hearth, two enormous logs crackling and chattering to each other.

Half an hour later, it was certainly time for a drink. Agreement had been made to abstain at first, so everyone could keep a clear head and proffer their thoughts, but having laid out the frankly surreal events of the last three days, it all seemed to be getting more complicated rather than less.

"I'm glad I have you two to run this by - get a detached perspective," Jon said. Angus had gone to the bar to sort the drinks. "Phil Mayhew and Lisa Grant have real evidence they can produce. Jason can too, but then some of that physical evidence doesn't make any sense either."

The SOCO, sitting next to his boss, leant forward, and looked thoughtfully at the three reports on the table in front of him.

"So, I've got basic forensic evidence regarding Frank and Brenda's injuries. They make sense. I have the same for Gibson's. He suffered no injuries at all, but Dr Mayhew says the situation he was in should have been completely unsurvivable."

"The museum and the library presented the rust, food decomposition, mould and dry rot evidence: some of which began to appear within less than an hour after I entered the scene. At the library, all the metalwork and woodwork showed the same - this was conspicuous, even amongst the fire damage. Even at the beach, it was the same: I found rotting seaweed within a fifteen-metre radius around the part of the sand-shelf they dug him out of: beyond that, it was healthy again. The metal chair frame was covered in rust, the sandwich next to it rotten, and his clothes riddled with dry rot: virtually falling to bits. He couldn't possibly have put them on in that condition in the first place." He took a bottle from Angus who was back at the sofa handing out the beer. "For the next piece of evidence, I had to phone a colleague at the oceanography faculty at Southampton University. I described what I'd found on the sand: colour, consistency and faxed him a couple of photos. He identified the substance as a marine mould. He couldn't pin down the strain, but he was adamant that's what it was."

Angus took a large swig of beer and said, "I didn't even know such a thing existed."

"Me neither," Jason continued. "And what makes it so utterly nuts is that this stuff grows on rocks that are submerged for the most part underwater. Not dry sand. The tide doesn't even reach that far up the beach. Ever."

Clara shifted in her seat. "Ok, so, some of the tangible stuff is relevant, the other is a common feature at all scenes but makes no sense as we can see it. If you put the tangible to one side, what are you left with?" Clara asked.

Jon shook his head a fraction. "This does my head in. Real-life is not like this. I've dealt with real-life incidents as a career for thirty years, but even so, this bizarre situation is right in front of my eyes. Jason's and Phil's reports relating to each victim's physical condition, and Lisa's, regarding the fire at the library. In black and white." He looked at Angus and Clara, shrugged, palms upwards.

Clara took a sip of her Jack Daniels, the ice clinking against the tumbler. "Go through each. At least this way we're grouping the evidence."

Angus nodded. "We need to consider if you have to actually regard any of the weird stuff and separate that from the pertinent evidence."

"There's more to it than that, Dad." Clara said. "But let's keep going in this direction first, though. Did any of the evidence have any common factors?"

Jason picked up one of the reports. "I'm satisfied that Frank sustained his injury from falling and hitting his head on the skirting of the display cabinet. Firstly, Dr Mayhew couldn't explain why it bled so much, and then why it stopped so suddenly: just at the point when any more loss would have proved fatal." He swapped the report for the next one on the table.

"With Gibson, again, it's utterly nuts. Surfers eventually found him. We don't know exactly how long he was buried in the sand: it was certainly a minimum of ten minutes. Dr Mayhew said he'd give anyone in that situation about forty seconds before they were unconscious, and around three minutes after that – dead. How in God's name did the old git survive that?"

"How the hell did he get in there in the first place – and end up with his feet hanging out like that?" Angus asked.

Jason picked up the last report. "Not a clue." He flipped through the pages. "Coming on to Brenda, there was nothing especially odd about her injuries, other than her staunch belief they were caused by objects flying across the room by themselves. She's got a nasty bruise on her head, but she'll be fine. It's Lisa's findings that sort of link up with the other two."

"Who's Lisa?" Clara asked.

"Our local fire investigator," Angus told her. "The only professional on the roster. The rest are voluntary."

Jason continued. "She says the fire, which started in the kitchen, spread to the main reception area, and the first couple of bookshelves." He looked up at them all. "And then put itself out."

Clara sat forward. "What do you mean?"

"The fire just stopped. Lisa said she can find no scientific reason why it didn't carry on and engulf the whole place, as she'd have expected. All that wood, the books, the paper. But nope. It quite literally put itself out. I did press her on the point, and she said she'd stake her reputation on it. What really freaked her out is this." He extracted an A4 photo from the report and laid it on the table. It showed a circle of carpet just inside the door of the library office, pristine, colourful, and clean.

The landlord returned, placing refills on the table, and picked up the photo. "It's completely untouched by the flames. How could the fire travel around an area like that?"

"Inside that circle, Angus, is where they found Brenda. Not a burn, not even any skin redness. Not a hair on her head harmed by the fire."

Angus dropped the photo back on the table. For a moment or two, there was silence. The sound of the rain lashing against the pub increased for a second, as a savage surge of wind rushed in from the coast, the rich smell of the burning logs permeating the air.

Clara began, "So we've got physical evidence common to each scene. We've got each victim surviving totally against medical expectation. These things, whether we understand why or not, seem to me to be two of three common factors." She took a drink, then

100

went on. "Then of course there's the third. The one no-one wants to believe, right?" She grinned.

"These 'supernatural' links." Jon sighed. He leaned over and took out the statements he'd taken. He glanced over them and a moment later, looked up. "Whether I like it or not, all three of them were unshakeable in their accounts of what happened. Frank saw the nanny fly across the display at him, causing his fall. Brenda swears she saw and spoke to her dead husband amongst the bookshelves and got hit by objects that flew across the room. There also seems to be no reason for the start of the fire. Lastly, Gibson says he got dragged backwards into the sand-shelf by the hands of corpses, but according to Phil, no marks on him anywhere." With a resigned expression, he handed the statements back to his SOCO.

For the second time that evening, there was silence. Everyone looked at each other as flame shadows flickered across each face.

Eventually, Clara spoke. "You need specialist help."

Both Jon and Jason shot her a look.

"Specialist?" Jon asked.

"You wanted an objective opinion. That's mine. You want answers, right?"

"I want to know if these common links might, in whatever bizarre way, have anything to do with the actual events, or if they point to some kind of third-party involvement, but hearing myself say that sounds ridiculous."

"What third party can be responsible for these kinds of things?" Jason pointed out.

Jon shook his head. "All of this has happened in the space of three days." He turned to his SOCO. "Utterly nuts, right?"

Jason nodded emphatically. "Utterly nuts."

"But like I said to Dad earlier, there's more to it than finding out whether these 'supernatural' factors can help to explain what's actually taking place. Surely we need answers that will help to stop anyone else becoming a victim? As you've said, three in three days."

"Who's equipped to help anybody with something this weird?" the SOCO asked doubtfully.

Angus grinned at his daughter. "Clara will know someone."

"I know someone who might be able to point us in the right direction, that's all."

Jon set his jaw. "I don't know, Clara. This is a small community, a close-knit island. I don't want this becoming public knowledge."

"You don't have any choice, Jon. What else are you going to do? Sit back and watch more victims pile up? Ok, we don't know if that's going to happen, but can you afford to take that risk?" She began on her second Jack Daniels. "Nothing you have here on this island is going to provide us any more answers, none of the expertise here or your own experience can help. Otherwise we wouldn't all be here talking about it." She met Jon's eyes. "Tell me I'm wrong?"

Jon dropped his eyes, deep in thought for a moment. Eventually, he looked back up.

"If you know someone who can help us, Clara, please get them here." He picked up his beer bottle and downed it in one. He looked back at her. "As soon as you possibly can."

FOURTEEN

He'd finally got home around midnight and just managed to get everything perfect: curtains drawn against a filthy night, the house warm, the standard lamp glowing above him in his high-back leather chair. And best of all, a tray on which sat a bowl of tomato soup, a stick of French bread, and a generous slice of cheddar cheese. Steam rose from the bowl, obscuring the view of the TV a little, and carefully, he brought his feet up on to the cushioned stool in front of him. He plucked the remote from the arm of the chair and was about to turn on the TV when the phone rang.

Of course it did, because right now, he couldn't be more comfortable. It didn't matter how late it was, there was some kind of evil entity out there, he thought, whose job it was to watch him 24/7, and whenever he was about to get settled, the second his backside hit the chair, it made someone call him. He let it ring a few times, and sighed when it was clear the caller had no intention of hanging up.

He placed the tray carefully to the side of his chair,

went into the hallway, and lifted the cordless handset: calling himself a total idiot, not for the first time. That was the whole point of a cordless phone, right? To take it with you, so it didn't matter if it rang the moment you were chilled out with a spoon of tomato soup equidistant between the bowl and your mouth - and the X-Files about to start.

"Hello?"

"Hi Ed – again." The accent always seemed to come through stronger over the phone.

"Hi, Dina. I'm sure you called me only a day or so ago. You really can't tear yourself away, can you? Even at this time of night?" he smiled.

"You are so right, Ed. What excuse can I use? The man of my dreams," she laughed.

"Nightmares, I'd imagine." He started back towards the living room. "Did you manage to shoehorn my rye-ergot case into your lecture?

"I did, and it worked well. Thank you for sharing."

"So what's up?"

"I'd like you to stump up about £190,000 to fund the next five years of my research grant please."

"You've got to be kidding me? Have they pulled it? I thought the university was more than happy with your progress?" He sat back in his chair and put his feet back up.

"They gave me the usual crap, but I'm reading between the lines."

"Intellectual pride?"

"Yes, and reputation of the college. Weak academic roots, according to them." She sighed. "Which demonstrates how little they know about my work."

"Have they even bothered to read your data?"

"Probably, but that won't make any difference. It's snobbery, Ed. You only have to look at my students: occult studies encourages an analytical mind, the practice of deeper questioning, reasoning outside accepted boundaries, the development of deductive debate and argument. That's to say the least. All skills that they can transfer vigorously to their other subjects, yes?"

Ed felt for her. "Bear in mind it's not the only university in the world. They'll definitely be others who have decent foresight: they'll see how valuable your work is and the development it can offer their cohorts."

"I'm hoping for this," she said. "I'm here until the end of the year, so I have time to start putting out feelers." There was a momentary pause. "Anyway, this isn't the reason to speak to you. A friend of mine called me twenty minutes ago."

"Another night owl?"

"Not at all. Which is why I called you straight afterwards."

Ed raised his eyebrows. "Is she ok?"

"Yes, she's fine. But I think you need to help her."

"What's happening to her that needs a call this late?"

"We've been friends since school, Ed. I trust her completely, which is why I know her situation must be urgent. She likes her crystals and her Glastonbury, you know. But Clara's an intelligent woman: starts her PhD next year. Inquisitive, but also systematic, despite all the tie-dye and black lipstick."

"Ok. Then if you're concerned, so am I. What phenomena is she experiencing?"

"It's not her personally. It's happening across the island she lives on."

"Island?" Ed repeated, surprised.

"She said it was too complicated to go into detail on the phone. But she said people have been hurt. Physical injuries."

Immediately Ed sat up. That was enough. He grabbed a pen and notebook from the coffee table. "Let me have all the details, Dina. I'll get my gear together and drive up in the early morning."

"Are you sure? I don't know if they are paying anything."

"If people are getting hurt, it's not an issue. That's extremely rare, and has the potential to become very dangerous. I can't sit here and do nothing, if there's any way I might be able to help stop it."

"Ok. I'll phone her back and let her know you're coming."

Ten minutes later, he was packing a rucksack. His stomach began to churn at the thought of a possible genuine case – after such a long time. He tried to push the idea away as he stood up. His personal agenda, as benign as that might be, must take second place to every client's needs. He'd always stuck to that rule. There was no reason for any exception this time.

He pulled his lips tight for a second, managed to bury the feeling.

But maybe…

No! Give it a rest, Ed. Shut up and pack.

There was a long drive ahead.

FIFTEEN

"I hope you don't mind staying here rather than one of the B&B's, Ed?" Jon asked.

"On the contrary." He dropped his bag, looking around. "What an amazing place." Ed now stood in the hallway of the Georgian manor house, the largest building on The Borrow: of elegant white stone, Palladian in style with a central domed roof, four tall chimney pieces, and grand columns under ornate pediments at the front. An expansive gravel courtyard led away from the entrance, eventually meeting the tarmac road that finished at a pair of ornate iron gates.

Although an ostentatious building, inside it was decorated with a sense of clean line and space. The original blue Lias flagstone floor kept the hallway bright, reflecting light from the vast sash windows on both sides of the room. The furnishings were in keeping with the house, original pieces, much of them mahogany and oak, but just enough in number to make the place comfortable. However, the overall impression was far from any kind of stately show home: muddy boots in doorways, hooks straining under layers of coats and hats, piles of paperwork scattered here and there, all indicating signs of an active occupant.

The owner, William Brooksbank had lived on the island for years. He was a man with many friends, and well respected by the community. Despite his enormous wealth and land ownership, he was always in the thick of it when it came to fundraising, event organising, and such like. He regularly offered out his facilities and grounds free of charge for weddings, parties, jumble sales, charity events and occasionally, even small concerts.

"So, you must be the investigation chap?"

Ed turned to see a broad-chested man in his mid-sixties, striding in through one of the doors off of the hallway. His dark hair (more dye than genes) had been Brylcreemed back neatly at the front, but the back and sides were making successful bids for freedom. He was clean shaven with a warm smile; he sported a paisley tie, handkerchief, smart woollen jacket and trousers that were too long, bunching up over his bespoke brogues.

He held out a large hand. "Ed Thorn?"

Ed took his hand. "Yes, indeed," he replied, wondering how many fingers the man was going to break before he stopped shaking it.

"William Brooksbank. Call me Will. Unfortunately, I own this monstrosity." He indicated their surroundings with a sweep of his eyes. "Sergeant Pearce has told me about all this fuss that's going on. In complete confidence of course. And I'm right behind you."

"Thank you, I appreciate that," Ed said sincerely.

"I don't pretend to understand a word of it. But what I do realise, is that there is a potential risk to this island and the residents, and whatever methods employed, we need to put an end to that." Much to Ed's relief, Will stopped shaking his hand. "Anything you need, you just shout."

"It's very kind of you to put me up."

"Not at all. Would have done so anyway, but we wanted to keep you out of the limelight, so to speak, so it made sense."

Jon nodded. "The community here are a nosey lot. And I don't want idiotic rumours spreading. I don't think that would cause any kind of panic as such – these are no-nonsense people – but it could well hamper the investigation."

Will laughed, and it reminded Ed of a delivery truck starting up. An encouraging sound – reassuring. "Right, so let's get you settled in, shall we?"

Will showed Ed to his room, then returned downstairs to leave him to unpack.

It was decorated and furnished in much the same way as the rest of the house, light flooding in from the tall sash windows. He took advantage of the hand basin and towels in one corner, stripping to the waist and washing. After changing his shirt, he put the rest of his clothes in a drawer, his book on the bedside table and went back down to join the other two.

He found them in the dining room, just off of the hall. It was like walking into the basement vaults at the Tate Gallery: every available inch of space was filled with either canvases or painting equipment. Frames of all different sizes lay about the room, some propped up, others on the floor, some on shelves and chairs. Most were oil paintings, all either coastal landscapes or seascapes. They were beautifully executed, and to Ed's eyes, done so by an artist with shameless passion. Amongst the scattered gallery, the two men were sat at a grand oak table (the only surface not cluttered with paraphernalia), chatting.

"Pull up a pew, Ed," Will said as he came in.

"These paintings are incredible," Ed said, continuing to take in the countless works.

"My guilty secret," Will said.

"You painted these?"

"Certainly. Which is why I keep them hidden away in here," he laughed.

Ed sat down. "False modesty I think there, Will. They're beautiful."

"Well, I don't know if I'd go that far, but they're most certainly my escape. I'd be lying if I said it isn't lonely up here on occasions. When black clouds gather in the old brain box, I grab a Size 8 Russian sable, and get to work."

"Jon told me you're very active in the community, though."

"Like a car thief, you mean?" He said with a short

laugh. "Well, the good officer is telling you the truth. But that can't always compensate for living in a place like this on your own – I spend most of my evenings feeling like a dry pea rattling around in an aircraft hangar. When I paint, I'm able to lose myself completely in the process." He pursed his lips, paused for a second. "Between you, me and the gatepost, gentleman, I very much believe painting saved me from an early grave. You'll forgive me if I don't go into details, but you're both intelligent chaps, you can work that one out."

"There are few people I've got to know well that don't have their own bolt hole, Will. Including myself." Ed said.

With a warm smile, Will said, "Kind of you to say so. I'm certainly not ashamed of feeling lonely, though. I'm just grateful I've a decent way of attacking it." He leant forward, his elbows on the table. "Anyway, I was just getting Jon to go back over this whole situation again to help get my head around it. But I can't, so I'm going to stop trying. My only concern is to help put a stop to any more such incidents."

Jon had explained Will's position in the community on the way back from the train station: his generosity and enthusiasm. But Ed had reserved talking in much detail about his own background, instead, waiting until all three of them were together. It saved repeating an introduction he had given so many times before, he'd lost count.

"But you understand the unusual nature of these events?" Ed said.

"I served in the British army for twenty-five years. Honourable discharge, rank of Colonel. So I've seen an awful lot of both bizarre and terrible things in my time. Never knew what bloody thing I was going to come across next. One of the very few advantages to that is it's given me a very open mind. As the Bard said, 'there are more things in heaven and earth, Horatio, than are dreamt of in your philosophy'. So yes, I realise that this isn't quite the normal ticket." He sat back into his chair. "So, tell me about your good self, Ed. What are you bringing to the table?"

Ed sat down. "First and foremost, gents, I'm a debunker. I'm not a medium, or a psychic, neither of which I believe in. I use scientific equipment and logic to explain supposed supernatural or paranormal phenomena."

Jon asked, "Have you been doing this sort of thing long?"

"More than half my life," Ed replied. "Initially, I had a very specific motivation for doing this kind of work, but over the years, I became more driven by the need to help people. As you can imagine, folks that find themselves in a position to need my intervention often have no idea where to find such help. That said, there have been very few events I've not been able to come up with an explanation for, but that doesn't mean they were paranormal: just that my equipment was maybe not of the kind or sensitivity to disprove them."

"I'd be interested to see your gear," Will said.

"You're more than welcome. I'll show both of you, give you a rundown on how it works. Jon gave me details in broad stokes on the way here, so I'll take a look at the reports and decide the best way to go about things. Owing to the nature of the events, and the fact there have been injuries, I want to get started as soon as possible." He turned his attention to Jon. "Have any of the phenomena continued, or got worse since it began?"

"We don't know. Neither Jason nor I have had the time to revisit anywhere. We've been from one scene to the next just trying to keep our heads above water."

"How are those who were injured doing?"

"Frank, the museum owner is stable. Brenda, who was at the library has some nasty bruises and is in severe shock, and Gibson pretty much the same but with no physical injuries."

Ed stood up. "We'll need to talk to them as soon as we can. First step though, is to go back to the event sites."

"And as I say," Will said, "you need anything at all, just give me a shout. This place is yours: use whatever you want and go where you need to. Breakfast, you're on your own, but evening meal is usually about 6pm if you're about. Cook is rustling up his renowned lasagne tonight, which I'm sure you'd enjoy."

"Thank you, Will," Ed said, "this is all much appreciated."

"I could take you to the museum now, if you're ok with that?" Jon said.

"Makes no sense to waste time. I'll run up to my room and grab my bag." When Ed came back down, a few moments later, the Colonel led him out to the unmarked, where Jon was already sat.

"I'll get the nick to give you a ring if we need anything from you," Jon said, as Ed got in.

"Understood," Will said, and gave them a brief wave as they pulled away.

A minute on and they were out of the gates, heading for town. They rode along in silence for a time, before Jon said, "I hope you can help, Ed, because I'm at a complete loss. I want to stop any more people getting hurt, but I have no idea how to do that." He glanced at Ed, then back at the road. "Be straight with me. Clara seems to have faith in you from what she's told me. Is she right to do so? Can you really help?"

"From what you've told me about all of this, I certainly hope so," Ed answered carefully. He looked at the police officer. "This is a very sparsely populated profession, Jon. Take out the amateurs and the charlatans, and there are very few people left who know what they're doing and are prepared to do it as a career."

"Meaning what?" Jon asked.

"I'm simply being honest. If it turns out I can't help, I don't know anyone to turn to who can."

SIXTEEN

What George Truscott especially loved about the church, was the grounds in which it sat. Hidden from the main road by thick conifers, access was via a long, narrow lane that ended in a small circular car park, and four small cottages opposite. Here, even before reaching the lychgate, he could feel the serenity and calm that always surrounded the churchyard: traffic noise seemed compressed, more distant than it actually was: any wind that cut across the island seemed unable to intrude here. And to George, the sound of birds within the grounds became more brilliant and beautiful, the colours of the trees and hedgerows so rich and vivid.

Even a morning like this, with its veil of grey across the sky and sunless horizon, was unable to diminish its vibrancy. The Church of St Michael was almost eight hundred years old: checkerboard stonework, intricate stained-glass windows, and bold flush work. One of two churches on the island, it enjoyed a small but regular congregation, looked after by the current incumbent, the Reverend Don Pritchard. George had been his verger for almost eight years, a position he cherished. Reverend Pritchard was a caring man, sincere and without ego, and nothing had ever been too much trouble, especially when George was first settling down on the island, trying his best to get to know the parishioners. As such, his dedication to him was unshakeable.

He stood now, at the entrance to the church, staring out. He regularly tended the grass, and this year, it was so lush, it was as if each gravestone had pushed up through a deep, green velvet carpet.

He didn't need to be here this early today, but it was no trouble. He wanted to be. He wanted to ensure everything was just right for this morning's service, to leave as little for Reverend Pritchard to do as possible, other than deliver his sermon.

Pulling open the heavy mahogany door, he stepped inside and switched on the high ceiling lights. At this time of year, the temperature was much the same as outside. The interior was modest: oak pews, unpretentious pulpit, neat flower arrangements (which George refreshed from his own pocket every week), and other than the thirteenth-century wall paintings on the east side of the nave, there was little else of note. But for all its unassuming decor, it always felt welcoming. Another reason George loved the place so much.

He was not, strangely enough, a particularly religious man; it was the sense of belonging, the fellowship and the human engagement that replaced any spiritual attraction the church could offer him. He'd never married and had no children. Until she died two years ago, he'd visited his sister, Harriet on the mainland regularly: though that in itself had always been a chore because of his health.

He had always been a chubby kid. His father had decided that life with a telemarketer half his age, and twice his IQ was preferable to one with a dowdy housewife, struggling to bring up two children on the pitiful money he brought in. On benefits, and Valium, his mother had done her best to raise them to be strong, and independently minded: but unfortunately this had manifested in George being told for every good thing he achieved, there was someone else out there who was better at it. This didn't have the effect, as his mother had intended, of pushing him harder, or making him stronger. All it did was instil in him a low self-esteem so embedded it might as well have been encoded in his DNA: a complete absence of self-worth that was exasperated first, by school bullies, later, by his university cohort, and finally, by his work 'colleagues'.

There had never seemed any chance of escape, of breaking the cycle and finding a way to deal with it. Relentless and as damaging as any physical assault, twenty years of such abuse had almost destroyed him.

Moving to the island had saved him.

Here, amongst a caring community, his friends and the mentorship of Reverend Pritchard, his weight didn't matter. His tight curly hair didn't matter – or his bad skin, or dress sense or his whisper of a voice. On this wonderful island, everyone saw past all that, took him for who he was – allowed him, for the first time in his adult life, to be himself – no, not just *be* himself, but to be *proud* of himself.

And, at long last, with this had come the ability to address his weight, a result of years of uncontrollable comfort eating. The mental relief brought on by his new life, finally allowed him to find the right mindset to commit to such a daunting task. Nineteen stone and two pounds did not hang well upon a 5ft 5" frame: walking for any more than five minutes was exhausting and he had to build in an extra five minutes to any schedule he had if it involved getting up from a chair - double that if it involved a trip upstairs.

So from July, he'd been following his diet without the slightest deviation. His GP had sent him to a nutritionist, and already he'd lost just over a stone. Although he couldn't yet feel any physical benefits, his self-esteem was blossoming. One day in the not too distant future, he'd no longer have his bank account shackled to High & Mighty.

Especially now Harriet was gone, the congregation had become his family. Reverend Pritchard was his family. And as far as he was concerned, none of them could ever ask too much of him.

Except Mrs Jowett.

Mrs Jowett from the cottage directly opposite the church.

Because Mrs Jowett was a bitch.

The only person who'd taken a very vocal dislike to him, never turning down an opportunity to ridicule or belittle him in front of the other parishioners. What infuriated him further was the fact that over the years, she had done so much good work - practically paying for a new church roof, sorting out its financial issues, arranging fund raisers and representing the parish at the town council. How could she be so philanthropic, yet treat him with such public disdain?

Even so, whenever hawking poison at him, none of the parishioners took any notice at all, and encouraged him to do the same, but that didn't make it any less hurtful. He'd spent his life at the mercy of such odious people, and had decided at the time, to take no more: especially from some dried-up old widow who wore knitted berets, surgical stockings, sported what looked like a wisp of grey pubic hair on the end of her chin and owned an emaciated chihuahua called Winston. And she spat when she spoke. Tiny flecks of white phlegm whenever she hit a hard 's' or 't'.

So many times he had come close to asking her to order 'six pints of your most scintillating and splendid, sweet cider please' from the bar at the golf club where he waited – but always stopped himself – that would be no better than lowering himself to the level of the bullies that had scarred his own life. However, he'd exacted his revenge in the end – and very effectively. Her irrational hatred of him was a moot point now anyway, since she was now dead: something he certainly didn't blame himself for. Absolutely not: it was just terribly bad luck on her part. He sighed at the thought of it – despite Mrs Jowett being a bitch, he still wouldn't have wished that on her, or anyone.

He began moving along the rows of pews towards the rear of the church, huffing after every second step, straightening padded kneelers with one foot as he went. When he reached the entrance to the small sacristy, he sat down on the end of the last pew. Closing his eyes for a moment, he enjoyed the peace: the cool still air, the outlying call of gulls, the undefinable smell of sarsen stone.

So still.

So calm.

After a short while, he opened his eyes and pulled out his 'to do' list from his jeans pocket. He'd allowed himself to dress in his ordinary clothes, rather than his vestments, knowing the kind of jobs he had to do. He looked at the list:

1. Replace older candles
2. Reset the altar
3. Hoover
4. Last week's accounts (rough)

He always started any job list with candle replacement: the church looked beautiful when they were all lit, their glow reflecting in the stained-glass windows, throwing soft coloured shadows across the stone columns and arches.

Reverend Pritchard had decreed the tiny sacristy too small for any kind of ceremonial use, and it was now used as an office: enough room for a battered grey filing cabinet, one-seater desk, photocopier, and a bookshelf across the back wall that housed most of the ecclesiastical paperwork.

He hauled himself up with a groan, went in and took out six five-inch-long candles from the bottom drawer of the filing cabinet, along with a large box of Swan Vesta matches. Before leaving, he double-checked the sacristy door was locked. It was the only other entrance to the Church, and in this day and age, with religious artefacts and collection boxes getting stolen on a regular basis, it was best to be sure. There was only one sets of keys for the church, and he looked after them with great care.

As he stepped back into the nave, he blinked, and looked up at the ceiling lights way above him. They were still on but now, there seemed to be a whisp-thin ashen haze throughout the place. He blinked again and looked to the window opposite. Grey as the day may have been, light still glinted across each stained fillet. His eyesight had never been great, but it was definitely getting worse. He made a mental note to get an optician appointment, and shambled his way to the altar at the opposite end of the church.

He set the candles on the floor, and began clearing

away the communion paraphernalia from yesterday evening – something he should not have left until today, but Reverend Pritchard had insisted he was to go home and enjoy a relaxing evening for once. The wafers went into the ornate mahogany cupboard tucked behind the column to the right of the altar, where he also checked the stock of wine: six bottles sat inside, which was good enough for at least another three months: so he locked it and returned to the altar.

He straightened the vesperal cloth, and removing the purification cloth from the top of the communion chalice, placed it carefully on top of the storage cupboard, ready to be washed later. He picked up two of the candles, took out the spent ones from the ornate brass holders on either side of the altar, and lit them. At once, the odd ashen gloom seemed to lift. He left the spent candles on the floor to one side for now, picked up the remaining four, and as he turned to begin his way down the next holders, he caught sight of her chair in the corner of his eye.

Mrs Jowett's chair. Her own rosewood chair complete with haemorrhoid cushion.

God protect you if you had the audacity to mistakenly sit there.

It was positioned at the end of the first row of pews, directly in front of the pulpit – her front-row seat. And now, whenever George saw it, the vision of the stone-hearted old bag jumping up from it and hobbling with her knees together towards the church entrance, both hands clasped firmly to her backside, came rushing into his mind's eye. That was his fault. He accepted that: that was exactly what should have happened, but her dying thirty seconds later was not his fault. It didn't matter that no one knew anything about it, as far as he was concerned, he was not to blame.

He started slowly back down the nave, replacing the remaining four candles, leaving the spent ones next to each holder to collect later when he began the hoovering. The warm glow of the flames made him smile, a feeling of deep contentment filling his chest.

He was particularly looking forward to Christmas this year: Reverend Pritchard had organised a trip to Bournemouth for him on the first weekend in December, and all the hospice staff – three nights in a lovely hotel, theatre tickets for the Friday night, and after watching the turning-on of the famous Christmas lights in the Winter Gardens, a meal at the wonderful Westbourne Grill House. Then leading up to the big day itself were all the Church events to get excited about: the candle-lit midnight mass, carol singing on The Lend in aid of the hospice, the children's party on Christmas eve, where he got to play Santa and give out the gifts, and the old folks' charity Christmas dinner. His smile widened – he was so lucky to have such an amazing life like this now. Something he had dreamt of so many times, but had never, ever expected to happen.

All the candles now lit, he stopped and looked back to admire the sight–

- and watched with incredulity as the candle on the left of the alter went out: then the one on the right. Then the next two along, and then the next. It wasn't even the fact that they were all going out in turn that kept him mesmerised: it was the way the flames disappeared that gave him the hideous feeling as if a bowling ball fallen from his guts into his scrotum.

They didn't die out.

They didn't flicker and choke and slowly die.

They just *stopped*.

All of them.

As if some unseen finger and thumb had snuffed them out.

And then, the drab grey light began to creep back in from around the edge of the church.

No, no. It was his eyesight.

Just his failing eyesight.

As quickly as his wheezing lungs would allow, he hurried over to the large window on the right. As he reached it, he brought his face close to the coloured fillets and looked out. As before, he saw unremarkable daylight and –

- Reverend Pritchard...?

He screwed his eyes up a little to try and gain sharper focus, chose a non-coloured piece to look through. Distorted by the undulations of the glass, the graveyard stretched and bent, headstones bulging, trees and bushes deforming.

As did Reverend Pritchard.

From what George could see, he stood on the far side of the graveyard, a few feet in between the statue of an angel and a stone cross – just staring at the church. It looked to him as if the vicar's face was completely expressionless. It was hard to tell, his face distended and warped by the stained glass, but it was definitely Reverend Pritchard, and he was motionless,

…and he was staring at the church…

…or was he staring at *him*?

Surely, he couldn't see through the intricate stained-glass from the outside?

George slid his face slightly to the right.

The vicar remained motionless -

- and when he heard the Reverend's voice calling behind him from the sacristy, another bowling ball dropped into his sack.

His head jerked around automatically, his heart thumping in his temples and he stared down the nave towards the open sacristy door, the view seeming to suddenly elongate as if he were using the wrong end of binoculars.

Immediately he looked back through the window - the vicar remained in exactly the same place, still staring.

"I haven't all day, George," the Reverend said, "Come in and see me, please."

Again, his head snapped back, and he caught a fractional glimpse of the vicar's head leaning out of the sacristy doorway before it went back in.

Like some demented human pendulum, his head twisted yet again to the window.

The graveyard was empty.

An involuntary gasp escaped him as he turned, saw that every candle was now burning with the ferocity of a Bunsen flame, high and red –

- and when he saw the neat row of six sacramental wine bottles spinning violently on the altar, a stack of wafers neatly arranged in front of each, he nearly shat himself.

He could now hear his heart in his ears, drubbing in his chest – could actually feel it as it started to kick into overdrive. Sweat began to crown on his brow, and he heard himself let out a kind of pitiful sob.

Reverend Pritchard stuck his head around the sacristy doorway again. "Would you move that colossal sweaty arse of yours and get in here, George."

The vicar had never spoken to him like that, but that thought perished when he saw it – sitting on her chair.

Simply unable to believe it was really there, he shuffled towards it, legs trembling. The fierce candlelight illuminated the small, circular mound, and as he reached out with his hand trembling, soft wool caressed his fingertips and he picked the beret up -

Mrs Jowett's beret –

- and dropped it with a cry, as if it had burnt him.

The vicar's voice came again. "George! In here, now. I won't ask you again."

The candles continued to burn ferociously but even

so, as he slowly moved along the nave, more intense, deep shadows began to crawl up the walls.

If he could, he would have run to the sacristy, but an agonisingly slow shuffle was all he could produce: the thought of the beret, and the weird dwindling light, the roaring candles all just feet behind him made his bowels curdle. Ironic, he thought, even in the midst of his panic.

He reached the sacristy door and stopped dead when he saw Reverend Pritchard sat behind the desk.

It *was* him. His facial features were faintly shadowed, as if he were looking at the man through thin smoked glass.

"What's the matter with you?" the vicar demanded.

George's hand drifted out behind him, forefinger pointing. "How did...I saw you in the grave...the sacristy door's locked...I...."

"Stop babbling!"

"But I saw you there...you were in the gra...then...then you were in here..."

"I don't know what you're talking about, and frankly, George, I don't give a damn. Just come in."

"But I don't understand. Please, Reverend, what's going on? The candles, and the beret? I'm scared. Please."

The vicar frowned, his face seeming to grow a deeper grey. "What in God's name are you talking about, you silly little man?"

"Why are you talking to me like this, Reverend? You've never spoken to me like this. What's going on?

Please just be like you normally are. This is all starting to really frighten me. I just don't unders–"

"I wanted to thank you for your letter of confession," the vicar snapped. "It was a despicable thing to do, and you're a complete imbecile for doing such a disgusting thing."

George tried to speak, but now his throat begin to constrict. This was so wrong. Reverend Pritchard was a lovely man – a kind man.

"What letter?" he said, barely a whisper. He could still hear the candles burning viciously out in the nave.

The vicar slammed his fist down on the table and George jumped, a trickle of urine escaping into his y-fronts. "Speak up you cretin!"

"Um…what letter?" He felt he was going to collapse at any moment. His collar felt hideously tight, and a pain as if an elephant were standing in his chest had begun.

"I presume you wrote to me, setting out in eye-watering detail what you did, in the hope that it would get you off the hook. That, despite the vulgarity of this act, I'd take pity on you and keep you on as verger?"

"I…I didn't write any letter…". The pain began to shoot down his left arm, and sweat was now cascading down his face. He reached out for the doorframe, but it didn't help. He began to slide to the floor, other hand grabbing at his chest.

"Yes, you did, George. This one –," the vicar said, producing a huge grin and opening a palm towards the photocopier. It burst into action, firing copies out at a

130

rate that was impossible – hundreds in seconds, paper flying across the room, spinning in the air, piling across the floor.

George slumped sideways, struggling to breathe. He yanked at his shirt collar despite the pain in his arm, his other hand still scrabbling at his chest. He had to breathe.

He looked up desperately at Reverend Pritchard, but the chair was empty.

As was the room.

The insane 'shaka – shaka – shaka – shaka' of the photocopier continued to spew out paper. He finally sank fully to the floor, planting his face in a thick pile of the A4.

And yet, amid this unfathomable pain and terror, he managed to focus on the words. They were in his handwriting, a detailed account of it all. How he'd got hold of the medical-grade Lubiprostone from the hospice, cleverly swapped wine bottles around, 'accidentally' dropped the chalice during communion, replacing it after Mrs Jowett's mouthful to ensure none of the other communicants got a dose, and sat back to enjoy the results. Even such a small sip of that stuff as the old bitch had taken was enough: within ten minutes, she was rushing for the church door, a streak of excrement dripping down the back of her right surgical stocking. She carried on straight across the car park, towards her front door on the opposite side of the road and stepped right in front of a Walter Gamble's car as he returned home from work. She'd died instantly.

And now they'd all know.

Oh, dear God, everyone would know, and they'd never forgive him.

He would have sobbed but he couldn't get enough breath, an awful panic gripping his mind, the elephant now jumping up and down on his chest.

They'd take everything away from him.

His friends.

His family.

His new life.

Everything!

And as his eyes fell onto his handwritten signature, he heard a strange sound – a guttural choke – and realised, it was the sound of his own lungs, as his heart began to shut down.

SEVENTEEN

On the way to the museum, Jon went over everything again in detail, from his call at the Black Dog, to taking Gibson's statement in A&E, while Ed made continuous notes.

The weather had continued to take a downward turn as it had done over the last couple of days, and as they pulled up on the promenade road they could see thunderous waves rolling in on the back of a high wind. Pieces of litter shot along the pavement, in and out of bench legs and around litter bins, and any notice boards with heavy enough stands to remain upright, still flexed in protest.

Getting out of the car, Ed pulled his jacket collar up around his neck, and grabbed two small items from his bag in the back, and gave Jon his laptop. The wind buffeted the officer as he took keys out of his pocket, and opened the museum entrance. They hurried inside, and Jon slammed the door shut, their world suddenly silent and utterly still.

Ed looked out for a moment: he enjoyed watching the

soundless weather from inside, found it exhilarating, making him feel small against the phenomenal power of nature.

"Ok. Here are the photos Jason took," Jon said, pulling them from his laptop bag. Ed scanned them, took in the thick coating of rust on all the metalwork, the mould inside the glass show cases. "It starts down here," the police officer said, leading the way down the entrance hall. They reached the Roman room, and could immediately see the contrast.

On the floor underneath each area of rust, lay reddish-brown dust. Ed bent his knees and ran his finger across a section of it underneath a door handle. "Rust, rather obviously," he remarked.

He took out a Leatherman from his inside jacket pocket, flipped open the small blade and poked at the handle. Rust came away in great chunks. He stood back up and looked at the photos again. "It's breaking down. One minute it's two inches thick, and now it's flaking."

"Let's take a look at the mould," Jon said.

They moved over to the first display case several feet in front of them. The mould both inside and out had clearly turned to a dull, blueish dust.

"This whole thing just gets more bizarre as it goes on," Jon said.

Ed said, "I've never seen anything like this, but I don't know what it has to do with what Frank says he saw: if anything. Though, it's early days."

Jon moved to one of the beams with dry rot scars and

ran his hand over the rough surface. "I can't tell if the rot has stopped in the same way, Ed, not without Jason getting some samples examined."

"I think we can probably take that as read," Ed replied. He took out items he'd got from his bag: what looked like a small calculator with a short steel ariel on the side, and a similarly shaped item with a row of lights at the top. He showed Jon the instrument with the ariel.

"This is an environmental thermometer. It simply measures temperature. It's commonly believed that supernatural events can cause temperature drops. In the past, I've found these drops to continue some time afterwards, indicating a possible scientific explanation."

"Have you ever found one?"

"No, but that doesn't mean to say the events are supernatural." He proffered the other instrument. "And this is an EMF meter. It measures electromagnetic fields. Again, it's supposed that spirits or ghosts, call them what you like, use background electricity as energy to manifest. Ironically, high EM fields can actually cause hallucinations – such as ghosts." Ed gave a wry smile. He switched on the EMF meter, and one light flickered sporadically on and off. "Nothing unusual," he said. He peered at the thermometer. "Nine degrees centigrade. Cold but to be expected in a place like this with the weather as it is." He made his way towards the Victorian room. "Let's see what readings we get near the nursery display, shall we?"

Jon followed, Ed in front watching the instruments

as they went forward slowly. "No changes yet," he said: then they came within six feet of the nursery display and the EMF went off the charts, screeching as the display fully lit. Jon physically jumped, Ed nearly dropped it, and they both stepped back.

"Christ, Ed! Does it normally do that?"

"Not at all. It does hit the high notes, but very rarely: and I've only ever seen that happen when I've discovered heavy electrical cables or power junctions nearby."

"Do you think that's the case here?"

"We can't rule it out, but this place is hundreds of years old, and as far as we know, all we've got around here are LEDs. If I had to make an educated guess, I'd say it's unlikely, but we'll need to ask Frank to be sure."

"Would the CCTV system here give off readings like that?"

"No, definitely not," Ed said.

Jon pointed at the thermometer. "Try seeing if there's any temperature change."

"Ok, hold this," Ed said handing him the EMF meter. He stepped forward again, and the temperature plummeted. "That's not even natural," Ed said, eyebrows raised. "Unless we're sticking this in a freezer, you just don't get drops that fast. Not in my experience anyway. It's down to two degrees already." He pulled out his notebook and wrote down the figures. "Might be an idea to come back later and see if the there's any change in temperature or EMF levels."

"Whatever you think is best," Jon said with a nod. "There's the bloodstain where Frank hit his head," he said, continued pointing at the skirting. "The final place he went is the kitchen."

They headed that way, continuing to see rust flaking on all the metalwork, and disintegrating mould. Entering the kitchen, Jon picked up what was left of the wall phone and held it out to Ed. "Apparently he heard his own voice telling him not to swear in this phone when he tried to call me."

Ed stepped forward with the EMF and it screeched again, the temperature on the thermometer's digital display plummeting. "I suggest we get over to the library, see if we find any similarities with this place."

"I'm concerned about the beach scene with this weather. Any physical evidence is going to get lost pretty quickly," Jon said. "If you're in agreement, I'll get Jason over there asap and see what he can find, then get him to speak to Gibson. I'll let him know what we've come across here, so he knows what he's looking for."

"Good idea," Ed said, "give him the same list of questions," and listened as Jon radioed Jason with instructions.

They made their way back to the entrance, locked up and hurried back to the unmarked, keen to get out of the hard rain that had arrived. It was less than a two-minute drive to the library further up the promenade, but it saved them a soaking.

It was still closed at Jon's insistence, and when they let themselves in, they found the situation identical – flaking rust, powdered mould.

"Let's see what we get with these," Ed said, handing Jon the thermometer. They moved to the shelving first and immediately got high readings. They found exactly the same when they got within a few feet of the office.

"There's more likely to be cables and the like in here, but if I'm honest, it's too much of a coincidence that these things are going off the charts when we enter the areas that Frank and Brenda reported their visual experiences. There's no doubt we're on to something there. What that something is, I have no idea as yet, but I'll set up the remote gear, and we can monitor it all from Will's place. We might have more to go on after an overnight vigil."

"I took their statements as you know, but I imagine there are questions you want to ask Frank and Brenda?" Jon said, as he began making his way towards the doors.

"Indeed, there are," Ed said.

"So do we set up your gear or visit them first?"

"Definitely the hospital," Ed confirmed. "I need to know more detail about their visual experiences: the solidity of the apparitions, colours, how far away they stood, and so on. Very often the answers give me a more probable direction to investigate."

"That sounds good," Jon said and motioned to the main entrance with a sweep of his hand.

Around ten minutes later they arrived at the hospital,

made their way to A&E, and found Brenda's ward. A nurse was leaning over her bed, closing the blinds against the hammering rain. The dense, gun-metal clouds made it feel as if the afternoon was drawing to a close, yet it was only just after midday.

"Dr Mayhew has said no more than ten minutes, Jon," the nurse told him. "And Frank is in surgery. It'll be a day or so before you can see him." She pulled the curtains around the bay.

"Thanks, Marie," Jon said.

"I'll be just along the corridor if you need me," she said and left.

Whilst making their way to A&E, they had decided that Ed's questions were best coming from Jon: Brenda would most likely react better to a police officer, than a complete stranger, who, as far as she was concerned, had no place poking his nose in.

Jon turned off his radio and sat on the large, padded chair next to her bed. Ed stood to one side at the end of the bay, hands folded unassumingly in front of himself.

"How are you feeling Brenda? I'm Sergeant Jon Pearce. I'm investigating what happened to you."

She looked at him for a few seconds, searching his face. "My money. It's all gone. It took my money." Her voice was feeble, full of sorrow.

"Who did, Brenda?"

"Whatever it was, but it wasn't my husband!"

"The man you saw?"

"It wasn't a man. It looked like my Richard, but it

139

wasn't. It was something vile."

Jon glanced up at Ed, then back to Brenda. "Did Rich – the thing you saw, did it look real? Was it solid?"

"It *was* real. I saw it!" Brenda's voice rose in indignation.

"And did it make a sound when it moved?"

"Listen to me. It took my money, burnt it all away. It told me I'll never see him again. That's a lie – I know that's a lie!"

Jon kept his tone soothing. "Brenda, we want to help you, but to do so, we need you to try and answer these questions. Did it make a sound when it moved? How long was it there for?"

"All my money is gone. Every penny."

"What money?"

"It was everything I had." She let out a quiet moan, so full of despair it made Jon shiver. "My husband, you see." She closed her eyes, and after a while, Jon touched her arm gently.

"Brenda?" She opened her eyes. "I know you said you saw what looked like your husband, that the fire started and you got hit on the head, but what did your husband have to do with this money? You didn't mention it before."

"Probably too shocked," Ed suggested quietly. "She was probably desperate for someone to believe what she's seen. I see that a lot. Other details take a back seat."

Brenda took hold of Jon's hand, lifting her head from

her pillow. "The fire! All my money." Her voice began to rise, her eyes filling with tears. "What am I going to do?" It was almost a scream. Her grip became surprisingly hard. "What am I going to do?" she repeated, even louder, her face beginning to flush red.

The nurse came hurrying back in. "I think that's enough for now, Jon," she said, checking Brenda's monitor. "I can't have her getting stressed like this. She's still in shock and we don't know if her head wound if affecting her yet."

Jon gently removed his hand from hers. "Of course. Can you keep me updated as to her condition please, Marie?" The nurse nodded as she began to apply a blood pressure cuff around the elderly woman's arm.

Ed thanked the nurse as they got up and they began walking towards the exit.

"Doesn't exactly throw any new light on anything," Jon said.

"Just very sad, all her money going up in smoke."

"Yeah, hideous."

The rain was still coming down when they got outside, and they hurried to the car again. They sat for a moment, the engine running, Jon waiting for the windscreen to clear.

Ed made a few more notes then said, "Maybe we'll get more from Frank?"

"I hope so," Jon said. "So, what now?"

"Pick up my equipment, then back to the museum, and the library. I'll set up, then we'll get back to Will's place and monitor everything from there."

The windscreen was almost clear. "Do you think we're going to find out what's going on here, Ed? As far as I can see, the more we look into it, the more senseless it's getting."

"Me too, but let's see what the overnight monitoring brings," Ed said.

As they pulled away, Jon's radio came to life.

"Sarge, you receiving?"

"Go on."

"Can you get down to St Michael's on the hurry up? The vicar found his verger unconscious on the floor about ten minutes ago. He's come round, and an ambulance is on the way."

"Do we know what happened?"

"It's not clear yet. But the vicar says that his verger keeps babbling about…uh…"

"About what?"

"Well…doppelgängers and uh…ghosts."

Jon and Ed looked at each other.

"Ok, we're on the way." He flicked on the blue lights and pulled away.

"Here we go again?" Ed asked.

Jon raised his eyebrows. "Here we go again."

EIGHTEEN

Jason bent forward and lifted the letterbox. The smell of stale body odour and burnt fat wafted out. He stood back up and tried the bell again. He'd not been to Gibson's home address before, and by the looks of it, felt he hadn't really missed out: a small two-bed semi, white painted pebble dash, now grey and flaking, battered for years by sand carried on offshore winds. The woodwork around the filth-covered windows looked tired, bits hanging off here and there, and he wasn't even sure the bell he had his thumb to was working.

The front door fitted in well with the rest of the house – no paint left on it, the number '7' hanging upside down, and he could see a small gap down the unhinged side where it was slightly warped. He bent again, breathing through his mouth.

"Mr Gibson? Are you in? I'm not sure if your bell's working." He could see a hallway, a door to the left further down, and what looked to be a door into the kitchen at the end, but there were no lights on and it was difficult to be sure. He listened for a moment, and when no answer came he stood back up again, letting the letterbox go with a dull 'clunk'.

He looked at the ground floor window, but the curtains were drawn, the same for those upstairs. There was a tall wooden side-gate to the left of the property, so he made his way over to it. He couldn't just wander in, but thought a quick look over the top wouldn't hurt. He went on tip-toes, and straight away saw Gibson, sat in his back garden. He tried the handle and found it unlocked. Opening the gate enough to poke his head through, he called out. "Mr Gibson. It's Jason, the SOCO from the police station. Can I come in?"

The old man visibly jumped, almost knocking himself sideways in his chair. He sat in an old wicker thing, a huge candlewick blanket with a stunning variety of stains wrapped around his whole body. Although, he wasn't just sat in his garden – he was sat in the very centre where once there had obviously been a lawn, now just patches of weeds. He didn't turn his head to look at Jason as he approached, only moved his eyes to follow his progress briefly, then turned his gaze forward again.

"What do you want?" he asked, voice wavering, high pitched.

"It's nothing to worry about. I know Sergeant Pearce took your statement, but he just wanted me to double-check a couple of things, if that's ok?"

Gibson grimaced. "Like what? You lot don't believe a word I've said anyway. What's the bloody point of double-checking that?"

Jason took the paper out of his pocket on which he'd written down Jon's questions. "It's just standard procedure."

The old man huffed. "Standard procedure, my arse."

"So when these things got hold of you – "

"Hands. They weren't 'things', they were hands."

"When they got hold of you, they came from behind, yes?"

"Yes."

"Did you see what they looked like?"

"Of course I did. They were all over my bloody face. They were repulsive. Arms and hands with the flesh hanging off. You could see their bones, for Christ's sake."

"So skeletal then?"

He shivered visibly. "It makes me feel sick just thinking about it."

"But they were strong enough to haul you backwards?"

"I didn't climb into the sand shelf myself, did I, you moron!"

Jason suppressed a smirk. "No, of course not. I wasn't suggesting that, Mr Gibson."

"It was like being pulled in by a bloody bulldozer. I couldn't move, I couldn't do a damn thing to get them off of me."

"Was there any kind of smell when it happened?"

"They stank, let me tell you. Bloody putrid. Like

rotting beef."

"Can you tell how many arms or hands there were?"

Gibson looked incredulous. "I wasn't exactly counting them, you idiot. They were all over my mouth and nose, grabbing my neck and my chest."

"But A&E said they found no marks on you, is that right?"

"I don't give a shit what they said. I nearly died out there. Those disgusting things dragged me into that sand and I nearly died. Whether they left marks on me or not is completely irrelevant as far as I'm concerned. I know what happened – as clear as day – and I've told you what happened. That idiot bunch of surfers who found me, they'll tell you! They'll tell you exactly how they found me, buried alive with just my feet sticking out."

Once again, Jason felt a smirk coming on, managed to hide it by dropping his head towards the list in his hand as if the writing were too small.

"Ok, thanks, Mr Gibson. That's all I need." Gibson huffed again, curling his lip, and turned his attention back to the middle distance.

Jason walked back to the side gate, was about to go through, then turned back. "Can I just ask why you're sat right in the middle of your garden, Mr Gibson? It's a cold day. Wouldn't you rather be inside?"

"Are you completely stupid? They can't get me if I'm out here. I can see everything. All around me. If they come for me again, I'll see them in plenty of time to get the hell away."

Jason thought for a second then said, "What if they come from underneath you?"

Gibson glared at him, a strange look of sudden realisation and chronic irritation. "Sod off you smart arse! Get out of my bloody garden. Just piss off and don't set foot in here again."

Jason turned back to the gate smiling, went through, and closed it gently behind him.

NINETEEN

Ed had to take a few seconds to compose himself when they pulled up at the church car park. He'd never experienced a blue light run before, and the situation aside, he'd loved it. It was like being a schoolboy all over again, grinning to himself, cars pulling aside as they sped through country lanes, then heavier traffic parting before them as they cut through the town. The simple act of putting his trust entirely in the trained driver beside him was liberating, a kind of relaxed freedom he'd never felt before.

Jon was already out of the vehicle as Ed let out a long breath and opened his door. An ambulance was parked next to the lychgate with its rear doors open, and a man in a black suit and white dog collar was making his way towards them in long strides.

"How are you, Jon? Thank you for coming so quickly."

"Afternoon, Don." He motioned towards Ed. "This is Mr Thorne. He's a private contractor helping me out at the moment."

"Call me Ed," the investigator said, shaking the hand that the vicar proffered. It was a firm, sincere grip, which surprised Ed a little, when he took in the man's gangly frame, long, thin face, and shock of grey hair.

Jon pulled out his pocketbook. "What's happened, Don?"

"Well," he began, elongating the word, his speech deliberate and steady. "I turned up to get things organised for this afternoon's service, and I found poor George lying unconscious on the floor of the office. I was most shocked. When I knelt down beside him to help, he started to come around, but he seemed incoherent. I thought he might have been attacked. He looked terrible: soaked with sweat, his face all red and puffy, so of course, I called for an ambulance."

Jon began making notes. "Was he able to tell you what happened?"

The vicar shook his head. "I couldn't get any sense out of him, Jon. He just kept going on about me being in the churchyard, and the office, which was very odd."

Jon looked up from his note-taking. "Why should that be odd?"

"Well, at the same time, you see? He kept saying over and over that he saw me standing in the churchyard and in the office at the same time. I mean, that just doesn't make sense does it? And I don't have the keys to the church anyway: but oddly, when I arrived the sacristy door was ajar. He kept telling me I had a doppelgänger. I thought he'd hit his head and was perhaps delirious."

Jon shot Ed a look. "And he didn't say anything other than this? No mention of an assailant?"

"I did think at one point he mentioned his belly, or maybe a berry – but I really couldn't understand him. He then started on again about me having this doppelgänger, as he called it." He gave a heavy sigh. "I really don't know, it was all very odd."

"Did anything look out of place in the church itself?" Jon asked, and for a flash of a second, Ed thought he caught an expression pass over the vicar's face. But it was gone, and was so quick it might have been nothing more than a subtle change of the light.

"I don't think so," he said slowly and paused for thought. "No, not that I recall."

"And have you been back inside since?"

"No, indeed. Once the ambulance arrived, it wasn't long before they managed to get George into it, and I waited here for you to arrive."

Jon flipped his notebook closed. "Ok, thanks, Don. I'll take a full statement from you a bit later. Are you okay to wait here whilst we speak to George, and take a look inside the church?"

"Of course. I want to go with him to the hospital anyway, so I'm not going anywhere."

As they walked towards the ambulance, Jon said, "I don't think Don knows anything of use to be honest, so I didn't see any point in asking him more questions that would just fuel his curiosity. The fewer that are involved with this madness, the better."

"Yeah, I agree. But we need to get a lot more answers from George at some point," Ed said as they reached the ambulance doors.

They found the verger sitting up on the trolley, blanket over his legs, wired up to a heart monitor. He looked like a waxwork: lank hair plastered around his face, and an ash-grey pallor that served to make the trauma in his dark eyes even more pronounced. Ray, the same paramedic who'd attended at the museum, sat next to him, placing a cannula in his arm.

"Afternoon, Mr Ellis. How is he?" Jon asked.

Ray connected a drip to the cannula and stepped out of the ambulance to join them.

"I can't explain it, Jon," he said lowering his voice. "The man should be dead." He motioned for them to move with him quite some way from the ambulance doors. "His ECG shows he's had a massive heart attack. I ran it *three* times. No doubt about it - no one could have survived that."

"But he did," Ed said, without too much surprise.

Jon held a hand out towards Ed. "This is Ed Thorne, Ray. He's a contractor helping me out with a few things."

Ray nodded to the investigator. "He certainly did. If I didn't have the readings in front of me, medically, I'd have no reason or indication to think there is anything wrong with this man, apart from looking like crap, that is. I've put him on fluids to be sure, but that's as much as I can do for what is essentially, a well man. His O2 is 98, his blood pressure is fine, his respiratory effort is fine. I don't get it at all."

The driver's door opened and Ray's crew-mate looked back at them. "You ready to go?"

Ray was about to answer, and Jon cut him off. "Can we have a minute with him before you leave? Is he up to it?"

"Ok, but make it quick. I want to get him to A&E pronto just to be on the safe side."

They returned to the ambulance, Ray climbing in the back, but before Jon joined him he turned to Ed. "Shall I do the talking again – the usual thing: he knows me, don't want to panic him and all that?"

"Please do. I'll go and see what we've got inside the church if anything."

"I'll meet you in there once I'm finished here." Ed nodded, waited for him to step up into the ambulance, and shut the doors behind him. The wind was now strong enough to start lifting fine stones from the grave and send them skirting across the car park. As he went through the lychgate, the treetops rustled, constantly creating a particular sound, along with the omnipresent call of crows that Ed only ever associated with graveyards.

He reached the mahogany door and went in. Turning, he grabbed the metal ring on the inside to close the door, and at once he felt it: the rough, lumpy surface, rather than the cool, smooth texture he was expecting. Looking down he saw the bulbous mass of rust encrusting the door pull. Almost simultaneously, the dank, slightly acrid odour hit his nostrils as he looked back up at the church interior –

- any metal surface or object he could see was coated in a thick layer of rust: candle holders, altar railings, plaque frames, collection bowls, hinges, handles, simply everything – and throughout the place, patches of purple-yellow mould appeared sporadically from the stonework and flagged flooring.

He could see the doorway to the sacristy towards the rear of the church, and began walking between the rows of pews to reach it, taking out his EMF meter and flicking it on. One light on the display blinked slowly and silently. As he passed the very first, he could already see the dry rot: and not a pew had escaped it. The EMF did nothing all the way down to the office, but the moment his foot went through the doorway, it screamed, and the display lit up with such intensity, he had to turn his face away as he hit the 'off' button. He looked down and from the marks on the floor and a few pieces of medical packaging left behind by the paramedics, it was clear where the vicar had found George lying. Rot had begun to eat away at the chair and desk, rust covering anything metal, but other than that, it was just a small office: large bookshelf, filing cabinet and a photocopier. Everything relatively in order as far as he could tell.

He heard the sound of the church door open and

looked up to see Jon coming in, watched as the police officer made the exact same expression he had when he caught sight of the sea of rust.

"I was going to ask you if you'd found anything significant, but I won't bother," he said, his eyes still moving around the church.

"How about this, Jon," Ed said. He switched his EMF meter back on and repeated his actions from a few moments earlier.

"Bloody hell, Ed," Jon said, flinching, "you need a volume control on that thing. You made me jump out of my skin again."

"Look at the pews too," Ed said.

Jon walked over to him, running his hands over some of them as he went. "The dry rot again."

Ed nodded. "Well, if there was ever the tiniest doubt that these features are just coincidence, you can sure as hell scrap that now." He looked down again at George's sweat stains on the carpet.

Jon ran his finger along the door handle to the office, a small cloud of red dust billowing in its wake. "Why in God's name is this stuff appearing?"

Ed chewed his lip for a second. "I wonder if it's some kind of airborne ingestion?" he said, more to himself than Jon.

"Airborne what?" Jon asked.

Ed looked up. "We've got two distinct things going on here. At each scene, we find the rust, mould, and dry rot, as well as all the witnesses claim to have seen 'supernatural' phenomena. What if it's something in the air that's causing both?"

Jon's expression was doubtful. "What kind of something?"

"Some naturally occurring airborne chemical, maybe - or something biological. Something that causes the rust and rot and mould, and has some kind of unintentional hallucinogenic effect on people if ingested?"

"Why airborne?" Jon asked.

"Because that would explain why it's random. I mean, a museum, then a library, a beach and now a church? No obvious connection between them. So, is there something the same at each place, some toxin or other, that people are unwittingly ingesting and suffering hallucinations as it begins to take effect?"

Jon shook his head. "I can see where you're coming from, but that doesn't explain why each of the victims survived 'unsurvivable' injuries. I mean, how does an ingested chemical substance have the ability to stop a raging fire from consuming an old woman?"

Ed ran it through his mind for a second and sighed. "I thought just for a moment I had the seeds of a scientific angle on this. I want it to be scientific because it would make some sense out of it, but you're right, it falls through completely when it comes to Brenda." He nodded towards the car park. "Did you get anything useful from the verger?"

"Nothing more than Don already told us. I could

hardly understand a word he was saying. The poor guy looked terrified. Whatever he saw, it was real enough to him." He looked around perfunctorily. "I think we should get this place sealed off and Jason down here to see what he can do."

"And I need to start getting my gear set up at the museum and the library. Covering the beach just isn't practical: I can't leave gear in the open like that overnight and expect it to still be there in the morning. And I don't have enough gear to cover this place tonight as well: that'll have to wait until tomorrow."

They heard the sound of tyres on gravel outside, and fragmented flashes of blue light cut through the stained-glass windows as the ambulance pulled away.

"Let's get this place locked up then," Jon said, producing George's bunch of keys from his jacket pocket.

They made their way back to the church door, and out into the fresh air. Jon closed and secured it behind them. Ed took a deep breath, glad to be ridding his nostrils of the smell of rust. And as they walked back to the car, he hoped that the coming nightshift would produce some results – because the repressed excitement deep inside himself at the thought he may have found a genuine case of astonishing magnitude after all this time was very much overpowered by the thought that, for the first time in his career, he was beginning to feel out of his depth.

TWENTY

It was bitterly cold when Ed and Jon had arrived late afternoon, the sky already a deep navy, the remains of the day's sun a thin strip on the horizon. Clara had got to the house an hour beforehand, and Will found her poor attempts to disguise her excitement about meeting Ed both charming and funny. Cook had left the lasagne simmering in the oven, and they'd sat in the kitchen at the large oak farm table, chatting over a cup of tea, enjoying the wonderful smell. At the far end, eager flames lapped at the hefty tree stumps in the substantial fireplace, periodically spitting out orange sparks across the flagstone floor. Such a blaze was needed to heat the large room, a size typical of the days when cooks and housemaids would have been bustling around, preparing sizeable meals for their masters and mistresses. At the other end was a double Aga oven, itself helping to warm the room.

The two men had come in carrying monitoring gear, Will had introduced Clara to Ed, then shown them to his studio opposite the dining room, where they all now stood. The layout was exactly the same as the other room, but in here, were not just canvasses, but easels, aprons, cloths, masses of brushes and paint pots on almost every flat surface available, along with four large arc lights in each corner.

"Shall I clear some table space for you, Ed?" Will asked.

"I've got my own fold-up desks but thanks anyway."

"Thought I'd put you in here as there are more electric points. I needed them for the lights so had a few extra put in."

"Spot on. Thanks. How about we set up the equipment first, then bring you up to date over dinner?"

"Much to tell?"

"You're not hoping for an early night, are you?" Jon answered. He put the gear he was carrying on the floor. "I'll get the tables, Ed. Anything else other than that?"

"Nope. I'll start putting this lot together," he replied, putting down the flight cases he was carrying and looking around the room.

Clara pulled up one of Will's painting stools from in front of an easel. "So Ed, how do you get pictures from the museum and library out here?"

"By going hungry," Ed replied as he opened the first case.

"Are you taking the mick?" she said with a sideways smile.

Ed laughed. "Not at all. I use high gain transmitters. Each site has one, and the cameras there are linked to it.

A master receiver here will pick up those transmissions and we can watch them on these monitors." He lifted a screen from the flight case to show her. "The transmitters are extremely expensive, so I've been on bread and water for the last three years. But they're essential. Without them, I'd have a hard time doing a decent job for anyone."

"Can you record your findings?" Will asked, stepping nearer, and peering at the equipment.

"Sure. Each of these monitors has a VCR built-in. I'd prefer it to be DVD, but the new recordable format and the players are way out of my budget. So I'm stuck with tape for now, but they're extremely high-quality machines. I get good results most of the time."

"Do cameras capture spirit activity, then?" asked Clara.

"Not that I've ever seen. As I've said to Jon and Will, I'm more a debunker than ghost hunter. The evidence these cameras have captured over the years have helped prove a scientific explanation for most of the phenomena I've come across."

Clara eyed him. "Ah – *most*."

"There have been cases I've not been able to debunk, of course. But that didn't make them paranormal. It just meant I didn't have the means to sus it out."

"And do you think what's going on here is paranormal?" Will asked.

"I'd be an idiot if I didn't admit something extremely odd is going on here. Some things could possibly have some scientific basis, but there's a lot more that don't – certainly not in a way I've ever come across. If I could capture something on tape, it would be a help. We'd all be able to see something first-hand for ourselves, something that may back up what the witnesses are saying they've seen and the speed with which this has all been happening is exceedingly unusual. Most cases I've worked on are slow burners: weeks, even months in developing." He opened the next flight case, began pulling out coiled cables. "And no one ever got hurt."

All heads turned as there came a clattering sound from the hallway, followed by the sound of Jon cursing. A moment later he came in, a large fold-up table under each arm. "Caught my bloody fingers in the hinge," he growled, putting them down, and shaking his right hand vigorously.

"Baby," Clara laughed and slid off the stool. "I'm going to check on dinner."

"Excellent idea, young lady," Will said and began to follow her out of the room. "We'll see you two in the kitchen when you're ready, then."

They made their way back and Will began opening a couple of bottles of Rustenburg Malbec. Clara checked the oven, scooped up a wine glass from the kitchen side, and stood in front of Will holding it out, a smile on her face.

"My dear, it needs to breathe," Will protested.

"My dear, I need to drink," Clara said.

"Hmm…" Will said, and poured her a glass, trying

to look cross, but failing.

Clara sat at the table, whilst Will began laying places.

"How long have you been painting?" she asked.

"Something I've done since my army days," Will said. "I'm not much good now, but back then I was awful. A two-year-old with mittens on could have done better. But it was a way to escape, you see."

"Therapy," Clara said.

"Quite, it's the age-old thing – when I painted, I was able to lose myself in it. Same as thousands of others do with their various hobbies, I'd imagine. There were days when you saw things no human being should ever have to see. Terrible, terrible sights. Awful suffering: pain, despair, loss: and often so bloody futile. Painting was my way of getting through it. I had a responsibility to my men. It was my duty to get them back home in one piece. So I had to be on top of my game – always – no room for dilly-dally. If I went off my trolley I would have put their lives at risk. Something I wasn't ever prepared to do, you see." He began taking cutlery out from a drawer, silent for a moment.

"Do you paint for the same reasons today?" Clara said

"Unfortunately, yes." He nodded towards a cupboard behind her. "You'll find plates in there. Help an old soldier and get them out, would you?"

"I think they're beautiful," she said, opening the cupboard.

"I think they're tripe, but it gives me a peace I can't

find doing anything else," he said, taking the plates from her. "I don't keep dogs anymore, and I'm getting on a bit. My dreadful daubings make up for all that, you see? Now, enough interrogation from you. Help me finish the table, would you?"

She stood up, poured herself a small refill and started with the napkins from the kitchen side.

They'd finished some ten minutes later as Jon and Ed came in and everyone sat down and helped themselves to the food, glasses were filled, and for a while there was a companionable silence. Jon and Ed brought them up to date as they continued to eat, and when they'd finished, Will sat back, wine in hand.

"Still don't fully understand what's going on, but poor George. Yet another victim of this bizarre charade. Have your discoveries given you a better idea of how to stop it?"

"Problem is, Will, we don't know what '*it*' is yet. We won't know how to bring things to an end before we identify the cause."

"Is the young man going to be ok?"

"It seems so. They can't find anything wrong with him physically, despite what all the tests are saying."

"Well, here's to the poor fellow," Will said, and raised his glass –

– and the house lost complete power.

If it had not been for the fire, it would have been pitch black: no standby lights, no socket lights – no external lights, not out here in the middle of the countryside.

Everyone was a smudged shape. And the silence too, was disquieting. No fridge hum, no low background buzz of electricals.

"Right ladies and gents, hold on one second," Will said, the sound of his chair scraping, then a drawer, then a lot of rustling. A moment later, a tea-light flame flared, then settled. Will placed it in the centre of the table, followed by six more, one at a time. Shadow mixed with yellow reflection moved across everyone's faces.

"This happens a lot around here," Jon said to Ed rather flatly.

"Quite the perfect lighting for what we're discussing, wouldn't you say?" Will laughed. No one else did. "Erm…okay then, I'll pop on out to the generator, get the thing started. Here." He handed Clara the matches he found in the drawer. "There are lots more candles in there." Clara began lighting, whilst Will took his coat and hat from the back of the door and took off a small keyring from its hook on the wall adjacent.

"Do you need a hand?" Jon asked.

"No, no. Easy as you like to get the old thing going. I'll be back in five minutes." He made his way through the dimness to the front entrance, put the keys on the hall table and pulled on his boots. Cursing himself, he hurried back to the kitchen, much to everyone's surprise, and grabbed a small torch from the same drawer as the candles. He hastened back to the front entrance, threw on his hat and coat, and went out into the cold.

The icy wind bit at his face, and he thrust his free hand into his pocket, keeping his head down as he made for the barn across the grass. The torch was good enough to help him avoid ruts and cow pats but, when he shone it up towards the woods at the back of his land, some four hundred meters away, it might as well have been turned off. He stared hard at the tree-line to see if he could catch any glimpses of a fire, but there was none: just the jet black silhouette of the woods against the horizon. He hoped Birdie had the sense to sleep at his own place tonight. He'd seen the small orange globe the night before, knew he'd been up there, but surely tonight was too cold.

Avoiding a few mud patches, he reached the corrugated barn door. It was secured by a large brass padlock, and he sucked in air as his fingers grabbed it, it was so intensely cold. He felt for the keys in his pocket. First his left, then letting go of the padlock, his right - both empty: and with a curse, he realised he'd left them on the hall table. About to turn, he glanced down at the padlock again, and was surprised to see it dangling open by the curved bar from its fixing. In the poor light he must has not seen it already open.

Right?

Yes indeed. Obviously. And his eyesight wasn't great at the best of times.

It hadn't been forced, that much was clear. He could only imagine he'd left it unlocked the last time he was here. He pulled open the door, struggled with it for a second as it bowed against the wind, and stepped inside.

The structure was no longer fit for its original purpose, and Will now used it for storage. From one side to the other, hand tools of all varieties were stacked up against the walls, and in rows each partitioned with low wooden fencing down the centre, decrepit pieces of farm machinery were lined up, resembling some agricultural graveyard. There were only a couple still in working order. The generator that sat in the far corner to his left: a robust Cummins 300kVA - you'd pretty much have to run over with a tank to destroy it. He shone his torch towards it, and for an odd moment he thought he saw the beam diminish - not its reach but its output – as if a grey gauze had been placed over the lens. He tapped the torch with his free hand, but it made no difference.

He swept the beam around the barn – everything was where he expected it to be: nothing out of place, nothing damaged as far as he could tell. So, he had definitely left the place unlocked. Early-onset dementia, he thought, without humour.

He shone the torch back towards the generator, stepped forward –

- and heard the dog whine.

His stomach flipped.

Not because the sound made him jump.

But because he knew the sound – unmistakably…

"Monty?"

The whine came again.

This was absolute nonsense. Will knew it; Monty had been dead for more than five years. But it was, without any doubt, Monty's whine. He'd had the dear old mutt for sixteen years, and such sounds were still embedded in his unconscious.

It came again, this time a little louder – from somewhere near the generator, or certainly that corner of the barn.

His face contorted with confusion, and a sudden lump in his throat. Will edged forward, sweeping the torchlight across that corner. He had to squeeze a little between the side of the barn and the pieces of machinery at the end of each row, and they themselves disallowed an unobstructed view of the where he thought the sound was coming from. He snagged his coat twice on the heavy-duty fencing, finally coming to the last row of machines.

The whine came again, and it struck at his heart. He brought the torch beam onto the edge of the generator, moving forward and to his right, allowing it to slowly reveal the very corner of the barn – and the dog curled up there, retinas gold as the light caught its eyes.

"Monty…" The words were barely a whisper, caught in the back of Will's throat. It was his dog. His gorgeous Monty, a thickset, tan-and-black Alsatian, with ears that never drooped, always alert.

"Oh my good Lord…this can't be…this is…" his voice trailed off as Monty gave another pitiful whine, hooked him with such a sorrowful look that Will could do absolutely nothing to help himself. He ran forward, arms outstretched, and the dog leapt from its corner with a vicious snarl, lips drawn back over glistening teeth, livid eyes edged white. Will instinctively threw up his arms in defence, hurling his head up and to the side, and he toppled backwards, hitting the ground hard.

At first, he didn't feel the pain - there were only silver flecks darting across his vision, a numb feeling as if someone had anaesthetised the back of his head and nose at the same time. He felt blood in his mouth, the thought he may have bitten his tongue roundly confirmed as suddenly the pain rushed in – head, mouth, back, but worst of all his wrist. He realised his right arm was over his head, went to bring it down to his side but the pain that lanced from his wrist, down into his shoulder, set his eyes bulging and he let out a bellow so deafening, he felt it couldn't possibly have come from himself.

Very gingerly, very slowly, he rolled on to his right side as much as he could, even the slightest movement excruciating. He strained his head back, and could just see the rusted, six-inch horseshoe nail hammered in from the other side of the fence, now protruding from his wrist, the end bent at ninety degrees. He stared at it in disbelief. How in God's name could the nail end have folded over like that?

He'd dropped the torch when Mont – whatever it was had attacked him, and without it, it was hard to tell how bad the injury was. But from bitter experience, he could feel enough warm blood on his cold skin to know it wasn't just a scratch. He hadn't been prepared to let panic shoehorn its way in – too many years on the front line for that crap – panic could kill you in such situations: raised heart rate, high blood pressure, clouded judgment, and foolish decisions that could result in disaster.

The second the hand-operated reaper started up at the end of the row in which he lay, his preparedness took a massive blow. He rolled flat again, pain searing along his arm, turning to see the machine. He'd never been a farmer himself, but he'd been around them and he knew what it was designed to do – sever through three-foot chunks of tough wheat, bale it, and spit it out.

And the bloody thing was in full swing, starting to roll towards him. He could see the handlebars, the throttle and brake cables - none of them were moving - but the machine was still crawling forward on its rusted wheels.

He rolled back on to his right side again, and forcing himself to ignore the insidious pain, managed to force himself up on to his knees, keeping his right forearm as flat as possible. He grabbed the end of the nail with his left hand, teeth gritted, face contorted with desperation and pulled with every ounce of his strength.

It got him only more pain as the end of the nail cut into his grip, without a millimetre of movement. He growled, a sound that erupted into a scream of unabated frustration, as again he pulled at the end of the nail – he had to straighten it, he had to get himself free before that sodding machine got any closer. The nail cut deeper, and he pulled his hand away, slamming it in a fist against the fence with a furious growl.

Maybe he could kick the fence over, but as soon as the thought emerged, it was pointless – he could see the thickness of the wood, the metalwork holding it together – not a chance.

The reaper was now a few feet away, and between the front guard he could see the blades slicing the air so fast they had started to whine. And as his mind frantically scrabbled for a way out, incredibly, he saw the machine move a foot to the right – its path now leading directly towards his wrist. He wanted to scream out, but gritted his teeth, point-blank refused.

He tried twisting around to get his legs out in front of him, thinking of kicking the machine off track, but it was impossible the way his wrist was pinned: he was twisted the wrong way. All he had was his left hand, crossing over his right.

He could feel his arm now drenched in blood, his head and face in sweat, the machine just two feet away. He thrust out his left arm, palm out, trying to line it up with a part of the machine he could use to hold it back. A second later the cold metal of the front guard slapped up against his palm, and the force of the reaper was incredible.

At first, he thought he had it – it juddered, seemed to stall for a moment as he pushed with all the strength he could muster - but it was useless. The machine drove in on him, and he closed his eyes, set his jaw in horrific anticipation of the indescribable pain that was about to consume him –

- but the sound of grinding gears and metal cutting into metal jolted open his eyes to see Jon and Ed, one foot each against the reaper, kicking it vehemently on to its side. The machine spluttered, sparked several times, but refused to die, the blades still slicing away.

"The hammer," Ed cried, pointing to a 5lb sledge leaning against the wall. Jon grabbed it, hauled it over to him. Raising it above his head, Ed brought it smashing down on the engine compartment of the reaper. Spark flew into the dark, the machine juddered, but like some kind of injured animal, it limped forward with small jerking movements, only inches now from Will. Ed brought it down again, and again, and with the third hammer blow, amid the sound of grinding metal, the reaper spasmed twice, and fell silent.

Will slumped, breathing hard and Jon quickly knelt down to look at his injury.

"I'll go back and call for an ambulance," Ed said.

"And the fire brigade. We're going to need something to get him off this fence."

Ed ran out, and Will looked up. "Not that I'm not extremely thankful," he croaked, his voice raspy and exhausted, "but how did you know to come out here?"

Jon smiled a little, held up a small bunch of keys. "We found these on the hall table. Thought you might need them."

"Thank God for early-onset dementia," he whispered, more to himself than Jon, this time, without a spec of humour.

"You need to keep still; I'm going back in to find something to dress your wound."

Will grabbed him with his left hand. "No, stay here. I'll need you if any more of these bloody machines start up." His grip tightened on Jon's arm. "It started up on its own, Jon. And you know me. I'm not some flaky fool prone to seeing things and that's not the worst of it." Will shook his head, his grip loosening again as he slumped.

Jon put a hand on his shoulder to keep him steady. "Go on," he said.

"That machine, Jon – that machine has never worked – not since the day it arrived in this place. It's been sat there, completely seized for more than ten years. And it's empty. Not a drop of fuel in the tank."

Jon nodded his head slowly. "Did you see or hear anything before this happened?"

"My dog."

"I didn't know you still had a dog?"

"I don't. He died years ago and I saw him sat in the corner over there, as clear as I'm seeing you now," Will said. "I know you'll think I'm wacko."

This time Jon shook his head. "You know, Will, not only do I believe you, but I'd also have been surprised if you *hadn't* seen something bizarre at the start of all this."

Will looked at him, eyes slightly narrowed.

"It doesn't matter, you just sit back and relax, we'll have you out of here very soon," Jon said quietly. Will felt desperate to sleep, and as the faint wail of sirens drifted towards them through the night, he lay back and closed his eyes.

TWENTY-ONE

The glow from the monitors and his large desk lamp cast a bubble of light around Ed, something he always found comforting, as if it were some kind of protective zone. The fire had settled down into a bed of rich red embers, still spreading warmth around him, and the mug of coffee on the desk steamed, ready to keep him alert.

In the past, he'd never been particularly nervous on his investigations, but after witnessing Will on the floor tonight, seconds away from a hand amputation, the reality of what was happening had really hit home.

They'd got back from A&E around 11pm, except Will, who they were going to keep in overnight: Ed had taken the first shift, Clara had gone to bed, agreeing to the third shift, as had Jon, happy to take over in two hours. Any doubt that they were dealing with a supernatural entity was now firmly ditched. They'd seen it with their own eyes. The physical manifestations now had to be accepted as those caused by the presence of an entity: Brenda's 'husband', George's doppelgänger, Monty, the supposed corpses in the sand shelf.

However, Ed had no idea why they took the forms they did or why had those events happened at those locations, and to those people? Was there a connection between them, or was it just the sites that were linked? Why were the incidents so violent? At the moment, he couldn't answer any of these questions, which worried him intensely. He'd been called in to help, and so far, hadn't been able to do anything constructive, or come up with anything useful. He hoped to God the night would produce something on camera or on the instruments that would begin to shine even a little light on what was happening. How could he stop this if he had no idea what was causing it? He'd been waiting for a genuine case like this for so, so long: and now it was here, it was a nightmare: frustratingly confusing and highly dangerous.

He was comfortable, snug and ready to sit back and watch for any activity, but his urge to make the call was tugging at his legs, making them fidgety. He looked out of the kitchen door and into the dingy, cold utility room where the leaf-green phone sat on the worktop. It was no good – he had to call – there was simply no one else to speak to who might be able to help.

Reluctantly he left the warmth of his chair and that protective circle of light, and stepped quietly into the utility room, suddenly feeling miles away from Eve's 'mission control'. He kept the light off, not wanting to cause any kind of noise or disruption, even though the guys were upstairs. It just felt right: considerate.

He held the handset firmly, lifted it a tiny amount, allowing the forefinger of his other hand to keep the black receiver pins down. He then put the handset to his ear, and very slowly lifted his finger so the pins didn't strike the bell. It was still an old rotary telephone, so dialling the whole number slowly to reduce the clunking noise took some time. Eventually, he heard the ringing tone, expecting it to go on for some time in light of the hour, but after the fourth ring, it was answered.

"Hello?" Her voice was clear, not the sleep softened tone he expected.

"Hi Dina, it's Ed. Sorry to call so late."

"That's ok, I'm sat in bed marking papers. So exciting for me, yes?"

"I'd swap with you right now if I could," Ed said with solemnity.

"What's up? Has it turned out to be something obvious? Boredom for you too, but in some cold, draughty old house?" She laughed, Ed feeling she'd missed the dourness of his tone.

"Far from it. I hate to admit it, but I'm getting out of my depth. And you're the only person I could possibly talk to about this. I'm hoping you may know somebody in your field who may have the kind of knowledge we need to sort this, and is prepared to put their academic neck on the line." He explained the situation to her, and she listened without interruption. When he'd finished, there was a second or two of silence from the other end of the phone. When she spoke again, her voice was notably lower.

"You have destruction – decay?"

"Very clearly."

"And these people, the manifestations they see are very personal to them, but in a terrible way?"

"Yes, it seems very personal."

"And – Frank, is it?"

"Yeah."

"He's not going to be running anymore? And this was his lifeline – his passion?"

"From what Jon was telling me, it's why he moved to the coast. He's been a runner all his life, and wanted to retire to a beach he could run on every day. He's had a pretty tough life and I think it was his daily escape."

"What about the library woman and the verger?"

"No lasting injuries. Quite the opposite. Brenda has a few bruises, and George seems to have survived a heart attack that would have floored an elephant. The Gibson bloke has no injuries either, but managed to stay alive after being buried for ten minutes under three tons of sand."

There was a sudden rustling at the end of the line. "I'm getting up. I am coming to you. I will be with you by midday."

Ed was taken aback. "Why? Dina, what -"

"- there's no time for that now. You trust me, yes?"

"Of course."

"Go and see the library woman and ask her more about the money, and the verger – he's not telling you enough. Something is missing with him, and the old man too."

"What am I asking George and Gibson about exactly?"

"I don't know, but I do know you have to question them deeper."

"What about Frank and Will?"

"We know about Frank, do we not? He loves to run. Now, he cannot run. And Will, he loves to paint. If you had not been there, he would now not be able to paint, yes?" He could hear more rustling, drawers opening and closing. "I know Clara uses a ferry to get to the island. Meet me at the terminal?"

"I don't know the ferry times, but we'll be there from 11.30am."

"Okay. And Ed – "

"Yes?"

"If something else happens again, be extremely careful. It is getting much stronger."

"What is '*it*'?"

"I'll know for certain when I get there. I have to pack and get on my way. I'll see you tomorrow," she replied and hung up.

"Bloody hell…" Ed took the receiver from his ear and stared at it, incredulous, eyebrows high. A second later, he replaced it softly to keep the bell silent, went back to the kitchen, sat back down, and took a sip of his coffee, staring off into the middle distance. Dina had never joined him on a case. She had to distance herself somewhat to protect her academic reputation, something they both accepted. So, the doctor on her way with such intriguing urgency, if *anything*, made him more concerned now than ever.

TWENTY-TWO

The figure sat on the edge of the bed, slate-grey light from the half-drawn curtains falling across the hooded face. It was cold in the house – always was. The heating didn't work anymore. The figure wore plenty of layers, along with gloves and boots

Damp crawled up from the skirting, and the single bed, unmade with just a blanket, had been pulled into the centre to avoid it. Posters of astrological signs, rune alphabets, Celtic gods and the like covered most of the wall space. On the wall opposite the window, a large bookshelf was stuffed primarily with titles of an occult nature – there were even rare copies arcane and insidious books such as The Codex Gigath, and The Munich Manual. The bottom shelf was the only one on which the titles veered away from such darkness. Here, there were only military titles, everything from the medieval period right up to the Bosnia conflict. The one piece of furniture in the room, a weary-looking chest of drawers under the window, was littered with trinkets: medals, cap badges, uniform buttons, small crucifixes of varying designs, candles, mostly white but several black, potion bottles small and large, hand mirrors, planchets, pocket watches, scrabble tiles, old jewellery, the list went on.

Yet today, the figure was oblivious to all of this.

On the figure's lap was an open paper – the local rag for the island. The figure's hand turned a page, trembling slightly. On the floor beside the figure were editions from the previous two days.

A foul odour of damp, old cooking fat, and mature dust pervaded the house, but the figure was oblivious to this too. Today's headline and the following story was all that mattered. Headlines from the last two editions were all that mattered. Frank's accident, the fire and now the incident at the beach – all connected – they must be. And if they were, that was a bad thing…a bad, bad thing.

TWENTY-THREE

They'd spent nearly half an hour with Brenda on the ward, being very gentle and steady, but finally, they'd gotten somewhere, and now they were on their way to meet Reverend Pritchard. When they'd inquired about George, he still wasn't in any kind of state to answer questions, still under sedation after becoming hysterical during the night. So, they contacted the vicar to see if he could maybe shine any more light on the incident. Maybe the relevance of Brenda's information would become more obvious after speaking to the vicar.

The weather had turned bitterly cold with freezing fog blinding the island since early morning, its thick strains swirling through the beam of the car's headlights. When they arrived at Carrie's Wood, unsurprisingly, the car park was empty. The Reverend had asked to meet them here whilst he walked his dog. Jon was sure he was speaking for both of them when he wished the venue were the vicar's warm front room, tea, and biscuits on tap.

"At least it looks like Dina was right," Jon said.

"Brenda's situation now seems to share similarities with Frank's: I'd have never seen it if we hadn't talked more to her about the money. In just that one small detail we've at last got some common thread emerging."

Ed shivered, pulling his coat zip up to his neck. "Why on earth did he suggest meeting out here? He can walk his dog any time, surely? It's bloody freezing."

Jon did the same with his jacket. "No idea. We'll ask him."

They left the unmarked and walked to the five-bar gate that led in to the woods, waiting by the Forestry Commission sign as the Reverend has asked. The mist hung in the tops of the trees, lending the woods an ethereal, foreboding atmosphere. Just occasionally, a murmur of wind threaded through the thick trunks, bringing with it the odour of damp leaves and mulch. It was not long before they heard the vicar's Volvo estate, and a moment later it emerged through the mist. He pulled up and got out, the dog conspicuous by its absence. He came over, hand outstretched long before he reached them, in his usual manner.

"I'm sorry to have dragged you out here, gentlemen," he said shaking Jon's hand, then Ed's. "I needed to meet you at a place where I wouldn't get visitors. The church is obviously no good as you haven't let me back in yet, and even at home, I tend to get unexpected callers quite regularly. I thought if I told you to meet me for my dog walk, you'd not think it so odd."

Jon gave the vicar a look. "Is everything ok, Don?"

"I'm afraid not. I knew straight away when I got your call that you might have had some suspicion that all was not right." He fumbled in his coat pocket and pulled out a sheet of folded paper. He took a deep sigh. "This was in George's hand when I found him lying on the floor. I wanted to protect him, the poor fellow. He's spent his entire life trying to fit in, trying to belong. Finally, he found that life, on this island." He handed the letter to Jon. "I'm sure I shouldn't have kept it, but I wanted at least some time to decide the best thing to do."

Jon read the letter, passed it to Ed, all the while the vicar looking more at his feet than at either of them.

"If this became public knowledge," Jon said, "and George lost his position with the church, do you think, as far as he'd be concerned, it would be the worst possible thing that could happen to him?"

"Without a doubt. If I'm truthful, Jon, I think it would tip him over the edge. The odd thing was, though, he kept telling me there were hundreds of copies, all over the office floor. There was just the one that I took from his hand. I checked the drawers, the filing cabinet, and found nothing. I also checked the photocopier, but it wasn't even plugged in."

Ed handed the letter back to the vicar. "I would venture that Mrs Jowett got hit by a car because she wasn't looking," he said.

Jon nodded. "George couldn't possibly have known that would happen, as stupid as the prank was. I can't see that taking this any further is in the public interest.

What would it achieve?"

The relief on the vicar's face was plain. "Thank you sincerely, Jon. You're a kind man."

"Finding out about this has helped us, Don, so thanks for being straight with us. We appreciate it."

"It's a huge weight off my conscience, I must say."

"I'd destroy it if I were you," Jon suggested, handing back the letter. The vicar nodded.

Ed checked his watch. "11:20, Jon. Dina?"

Jon nodded. "We've got to go, Don. There's nothing else you need to tell us, is there?" he asked steadily.

"No, no I assure you. Thank you for being so understanding."

"I'll get Jason to check the church today and if he's happy, I'll have it released back to you."

"That would be excellent," the vicar smiled. Both men shook hands with him again and walked back to the car. Ed was glad to get out of the cold and opened the vents for some warm air on his feet.

As they pulled away, he watched the vicar, saw him start to raise his hand to wave, but then drop it back to his side, as if he simply didn't have the energy to finish the motion.

TWENTY-FOUR

The mist still hung heavy in the air when the ferry arrived at 1:.45am. A couple of miles out to sea, the sorrowful sound of fog-horns drifted in on an uneasy wind. Only two or three weeks ago, the small ferry was still at seventy per cent capacity, but as the ramp came down, only four cars rolled off.

One of them was a metallic racing green Mini Cooper S, which Ed immediately recognised as Dina's. It pulled slowly into the terminal car park, and Ed, standing next to the unmarked, gave her a wave. She pulled up parallel and dropped the passenger window.

"Hi Ed. Is everyone okay?"

"Will's back home, all bandaged up but he's ok. Everyone else is fine. How was the journey?"

"Tiring. Hang on a second." She put the window up, unbuckled, and stepped out of the car, buttoning her black overcoat, and pulling on a white chunky knit hat with a fluffy bobble.

Ed chuckled. "Very chic – that definitely says 'doctor' to me. But you know fashion, right?"

She parodied his laugh, pulling a face. "I know how to keep warm, is correct," she said.

"Jump in," Ed said, opening the back door of the unmarked for her. He got in himself and twisted in his seat to face her. "This is Sergeant Jon Pearce, the chap I told you all about."

Dina smiled. "He's nowhere near as ugly as you described."

"Funny," Ed said with a straight face.

"Good to meet you, Sergeant," Dina said, offering her hand.

"And you. Please call me Jon," he said shaking it.

"Did you speak to the library lady and the verger?" she asked.

"Yeah," Jon said, "and we think we've found a common element."

Ed continued. "Brenda used all her savings to organise the repatriation of her husband who died on a trip to see his father in Australia, who had end-stage cancer. Ironically, he outlived his son. She doesn't have a penny left by all accounts. All she wanted was her husband back, so she could bury him and say goodbye. He was her entire life – nothing else mattered to her except him. And for her to watch that money go up in flames, knowing she would never be able to bring him home, was the worst possible thing that could happen to her right now."

"I'm sure she'll probably be able to get help," Jon said, "but at this precise moment, her whole world has collapsed. All she is feeling is pain and despair."

"So very bad for her," Dina sighed. "What about the verger?"

Jon nodded. "Same again. We had to talk to his boss, Reverend Pritchard, as George is still under sedation. He's so disturbed by what happened to him – or more by what *might* happen to him – that he's hysterical if he's not dosed up. But like Brenda, it all hinges on them being placed in a position that just couldn't be worse – their own personal hell."

"This is what I expected, and beginning to confirm what I thought when you described the situation on the phone, Ed."

"The vicar showed us a letter that was in George's hand when he found him unconscious," Ed explained. "To cut a long story short, the bloke played a prank on a rather embittered old lady who was bullying him, and in her rush to get home as a consequence, she got hit by a car and killed. It was just an unlucky set of circumstances, and George certainly didn't plan for it to happen. The letter was a handwritten confession, which he presumed would spell the end of his life on the island once the vicar saw it. He was adamant that he hadn't written it, but it's definitely his handwriting."

"I know him fairly well," Jon said. "He'd never found somewhere he felt he belonged until he got here. From what he told me of his past, for him, this place is paradise. And that's the connection: Frank, running was his life, Brenda, her husband was her life, George , the

Church and Will has his painting: and he'd have no hand if we hadn't got there where we did: four people left to wallow in their own personal hells, one: a lucky escape, although George's letter will go no further. He'll be fine once he's over the shock."

Dina nodded gravely. "Which is why they all survived their injuries, or were spared any in Brenda's case. They are forced to live now, with no choice but to suffer so badly."

"But Gibson seems to be the odd one out," Jon said. "He survived certain suffocation, but as far as we know, that's it. No personal nightmare."

"Which is a shame," Ed said.

"He's the paedophile?"

"Suspected," Jon said. "I know it the same as everyone else on this island, but proving it, is an entirely different matter."

"So think like this," Dina said. "What would be hell for this man? What would be the worst possible thing that could happen to him other than death?"

"Getting caught."

"So like the verger, finding some kind of confession, or evidence maybe, yes?"

"Yeah. He'd end up in segregation, watching over his shoulder for what's left of his life. Definitely a personal nightmare."

Dina thought for a moment then said, "Brenda had her money with her, yes? I wonder if this man had anything with him of relevance when he was pulled in to the sand shelf?"

"A fold-up chair, plastic lunch box, binoculars. A rotting sandwich," Jon said.

"And the QV-10" Ed added.

"The what?" Dina asked.

"A digital camera. Latest model. Very nice," Ed said.

"Did you check it?"

Jon frowned. "No. It didn't even cross my mind. Why would we have?"

"Check it, Jon."

"Ok," he replied, shrugging slightly, "I'll get Jason to do it now." He stepped out of the car, shut the door, and started on his radio.

"Thank you so much for coming, Dina," Ed said, "but I'm extremely surprised. Are you sure you're happy doing this? What about the university?"

"We'll wait to see what Jon's colleague says about the camera. But I'm sure I know what this is and if so, the university is of no importance right now. They don't intend to support me anymore, so I do not care for them. Nothing is of importance, only stopping it."

"I wish you'd tell me what '*it*' is. You're starting to get irritating." Ed said with a small smile.

"I'll let you know when I know for sure. Who else other than Clara knows of this?"

"Just her dad, and Jason."

"Who is he?"

"Scenes of crime technician. He was in it from the very start. We could hardly hide it from him, and in fact, he's been a great help. There's the local rag as well: we managed to keep Gibson's incident under wraps. They reported Frank's accident, the fire at the library and George's collapse, but as just that. They don't have any knowledge of what's going on. Jon managed to keep the scenes sealed off, and gave them enough for a story and to satisfy their curiosity. They seem like a decent lot: not exactly hardcore paparazzi."

Jon opened the door. "He's checking right now. Everything was taken into evidence after it happened, even his clothing from the hospital. The camera's in the storeroom, so we should know if anything's on it in just a minute." He sat back inside and shut the door.

"From the way Clara talks about these islands, this is a beautiful place," Dina said. "It is sad to know such a thing is happening here."

Jon nodded. "I'm just glad the tourist season is over. It would have been so much worse to deal with, and could have affected a lot more people, I imagine."

"This is right, Jon." The doctor wiped the mist from her window with the back of her hand. "The weather – has it been good?"

"Cold but bright. It's got crappy over the last few days."

Dina nodded. "Okay. This is probably right too. By the way, do I need to book a hotel?"

"You can stay at Will's with us. It's a big old place. What do you mean, 'probably right?'" Jon asked.

"That's kind of Will," she said, then carried on,

ignoring Jon's question. "At each place there was the rotting – wood, plaster, metal, food. That happened the same?"

"Most definitely," Jon said, letting his question go for now. "It was the one aspect that we never doubted – it was always right in front of our eyes." He opened his mouth to carry on, but the radio kicked into life, cutting him off.

"Sarge from Jason?"

"Go ahead."

"I've found photos on the camera."

"Anything significant?"

"Are you free to speak?"

"Yes, go on."

"Christ, Jon, they're all God awful. Kids – time-stamped and dated. And the name of each kid in the photo etched at the bottom. I've never seen that before. Didn't even know you could do that."

"You can't," Ed said. "Not to my knowledge, and cameras are my thing."

"What sort of photos?" Jon asked slowly.

"The sort I never want to set eyes on again. The memory card can store about ninety to a hundred photos."

"Jesus. Are you saying there are that many victims?"

"Not as such. There must be twenty or thirty of each kid, recording each offence in detail. Every step of it. Christ, it's disgusting."

"What do you mean, 'not as such'?"

"Like I said, there should be a maximum of a hundred on that camera."

"Ok."

There was a pause. "There are five hundred and forty: just not possible on a card this size. How can this happen? And I've done the maths. We're looking at eighteen victims, at a minimum."

Jon couldn't answer for a moment, and Jason must have sensed it as the airwaves remained quiet. "Ok, Jason. Thanks. Can you get it off to the lab on the mainland as soon as possible please? I'll arrest him this afternoon."

"Ok, Jon, will do."

The police officer looked at the doctor. "He's about to enter his own very personal hell now, Dina, that I guarantee you," he said.

"That's all four of them, now – " Ed said.

"It is," Dina said. She opened the car door, about to step out. "And now we need to work hard and fast to stop any more people entering theirs."

TWENTY-FIVE

Jon vaulted the dead oak one-handed as he saw the tails of the great-coat disappear amongst the trees eighty feet ahead. When he'd got to the house, there had been no answer. But the minute he shouted through the letterbox, threatening to kick the door in if Gibson didn't answer, he'd heard the sound of running feet from the back garden. He'd darted to the side gate and found it locked. In an instant, he'd kicked it open, and caught a glimpse of Gibson darting through the leylandii at the rear of the garden. Jon thought the man was surprisingly agile for someone supposedly in their seventies, but he'd had his suspicions for a while – something about the man's eyes – too keen and their colour too bright for a man of that age.

He sprinted after him, across the lawn and past a single garden chair, radio knocking against his chest from his inner pocket with his pulse pounding in his temples. The idiot wasn't getting off the island anyway – he'd put Special Constables at the ferry terminal, so unless he fancied a refreshing swim, he had nowhere to go. It was Gibson's instinctive reaction to run because he was scared, which Jon liked. It was about time he was scared – all these years terrifying others who had no power to do anything about it, it was his turn to be petrified.

A second later he smashed through a thicket and out into a wide path with pine trees on either side. Gibson was fifty feet in front of him, his gait losing stability, turning his head every couple of seconds to see how close the police officer was getting.

Jon was closing on him fast, and then suddenly, Gibson turned too far round, tripped on his own feet, and fell backwards, skidding to a stop. Within seconds, though he had scrambled to his feet, his hand fishing inside his great-coat. Jon would have been on top of him, but experience tapped him hard on the shoulder, and he pulled up sharply, stopping a good ten feet away. Slowly, he slid his hand to the back of his belt onto the handle of his retractable baton.

Gibson's hand came out of his great-coat, clutching an eight-inch kitchen knife, and he grinned.

"Never thought you'd have a problem with me, did you, Sergeant? Not quite the feeble old man you thought. I've diverted a lot of suspicion away from myself this way. Islanders – all of them such imbeciles and so bloody gullible."

"Don't flatter yourself, Gibson. Now put the knife down. I'm only going to warn you once."

Gibson laughed, his head back, his fillings showing,

but his eyes still on Jon. "What are you going to do – hit an old man? An old man who thought he was being chased by a stranger? An old man who was just defending himself?"

"Nope – but beating the shit out of a paedophile who was trying to resist arrest, armed with a bladed weapon, yes." Jon moved his hand slowly from the handle of his baton to the CS spray holster next to it instead.

"Paedophile? My actions are expressions of love – consent was never an issue. I show my children love and affection that society takes it upon itself to consider wrong. Who are they to say what's wrong and what's right?"

Jon's face darkened, his eyes like stone and he moved his hand back to the baton handle: this putrid specimen deserved more than CS spray. His voice was low, almost a growl. "Put the knife down you piece of shit."

"Come on, Mr Policeman. Let's see how brave you really are. As brave as me? I'm a man who is prepared to demonstrate the truth – to show love in a way that is pure and natural, against the tide of opinions from a self-righteous and pious society. That's bravery, Sergeant."

Jon said no more, simply started forward, hand still on his baton. Gibson didn't move, began waving the knife around, slashing at the air.

"Come on then, Mr Policeman – Mr Tin Pot Policeman on his tin pot island."

Jon carried on towards him. "You're the brave one,

Gibson? Let's see what you can do when your victim can fight back." The police officer kept his eyes fixed, not on Gibson's knife, or his hand, but his eyes – which gave him the immediate cue a fraction of a second before Gibson made his move.

The old man raised the knife and lunged in fast with a downward strike, but already, Jon had stepped to his left, far enough to allow the knife to cut through thin air but close enough to slide in and redirect Gibson's arm with his left hand, and whipping out the baton, the motion racking it up to its full length, he swung it up with all his might into the man's groin.

The strike was so hard it almost lifted Gibson off his feet, his scream so loud it echoed off of the very tops of the trees. The knife clattered to the ground as he thrust his hands between his legs and collapsed to his knees.

Jon brought the baton hammering down again across the back of the man's ribs with a snarl, and Gibson fell flat on his face howling. Jon raised it again, about to bring it down on the back of the man's skull, the thought of all those victims racing through his head, but at the very last second, he pulled it. Turning away he gave a frustrated curse. He closed his eyes, taking a few seconds to bring himself back down, and turned back.

"Ernest Gibson, I'm arresting you on suspicion of sexual activity with a child under thirteen, inciting a child to engage in sexual activity, and rape. You don't have to say anything but what you do say may be given in evidence."

He looked down at the pathetic man on the ground. "You're going to enjoy prison, Gibson," he said. "Spending the rest of your life looking over your shoulder, waiting for the shank between your ribs, the sound of the cell door being opened at night to let in some special guests, keen to welcome you in their own particular way."

"You've got to prove it yet, Sergeant," Gibson groaned, rolling on to his back, hands still between his legs, just about pushing a smile through the agony.

"You should have checked your camera, old man. But then, why would you have?" He pulled his own frank smile. "We've got everything we need. Every last possible detail."

Gibson looked up at him, eyes wide. "I don't believe you. I've been way too careful. I've left you idiots nothing."

Jon pulled his quick-cuffs from his belt. "Turn on to your stomach – put your hands behind your back."

"Go to hell," Gibson spat.

Jon grabbed his arm and threw him over, began cuffing him.

"I never thought I'd say it but there's actually one decent thing to have come out of this nightmare," he said.

"What the hell are you talking about?" Gibson moaned.

"I finally get to nick you, you piece of shit." He closed the cuffs on him tight, and the old man let out another groan. "Any reply to caution?"

"Screw you," Gibson spat.

"Nope," Jon stood up. "Screw you," he said and kicked Gibson as hard as he could in the guts.

TWENTY-SIX

Late evening, and Jon, Ed, Dina, Clara, and Angus sat around the kitchen table, the fire relit. Will sat in an armchair brought in from the sitting room, wore a short cast, and cradled a large wine in the other hand. Thankfully, the nail had slid between muscle and bone, missing any major nerves or blood vessels. He'd been given tramadol because the pain was still severe, and physiotherapy appointments running until February.

"Don't think we'll get much out of you tonight, mixing alcohol with those painkillers," Angus said smiling.

"You know you're addressing a decorated colonel, don't you?" Will said. "It'll take a damn sight more to knock me off my perch than that." He raised his glass to Angus and grinned. He looked across at Dina. "Thank you for coming to help us, young lady. It all seems to be getting out of hand, somewhat."

"It was very necessary. Not something I could have ignored when I heard what Ed had to say to me on the phone." She looked out of the window. "Do you always get fog like this? It hasn't lifted, even now."

"We get more than our fair share being an island," Jon said, following her gaze, "but it doesn't usually hang around like this. A few days ago, it was still bright – cold, but sunny."

"This, I think, makes sense," Dina said. The wind had calmed very little, kicking up loose foliage and detritus, sending it skirting across the grounds of the house in sporadic directions. From the kitchen window, the barn could just be seen, now caked in a thick layer of rust, the wooden supports scarred by dry rot. Will hadn't seen it, and the general consensus was to keep it that way. There seemed no point in adding to his trauma, and they all knew that in a few hours, it would begin to disappear.

Suddenly a plastic bin lid slammed into the window, making everyone jump, sticking to the pane for a second, before being ripped away again by the wind.

All eyes turned back to Ed who had his notes in front of him, and after flicking through a few pages said, "I think we've told you everything, Dina, other than the fact we got no results on the monitoring equipment except the rust continuing to break up. I'd imagine the mould and dry rot will be disappearing as well, but the cameras wouldn't pick that up."

Dina chewed her bottom lip, thoughtfully. "When I was young, around twelve, thirteen maybe" she said after a moment, "my father would tell me stories about his work 'battling demons'. I found them exciting and loved to hear them, but I didn't believe them: although I let my father think I did. During the day he was an engineer for an armaments company, but he was also a lay preacher. He would go away for a couple of weeks at a time quite regularly, but not for work with the factory. I was surprised they let him have this time away. We're talking the sixties, when the government was, shall we say, extremely keen on a strong work ethic." She took a sip of her wine. "When I reached sixteen, he told me more about what he did.

"He belonged to a branch of Christianity that went back deep into Ukrainian history, rumoured to hold knowledge given to the founders directly by God. I don't believe that, particularly, but certainly the texts give credence to the power wielded by this sect. They were good people, by all accounts using it to protect the populous from dark forces: but in great secrecy. They did not want such divine knowledge falling into the wrong hands as you can imagine.

"Their speciality was 'Pidtrymuyuchy Svitlo'– Maintaining The Light. My father told me he was particularly good at it. He was asked to travel to many places to do this and told me it was extremely important work that not many could do. He would take his good friend with him on these occasions: an ordained priest. 'Good old fashioned back up' he called it. Obviously, I asked him what Maintaining The Light meant." She stopped, gave herself a moment. No one said a word, all eyes on the doctor.

"Religions across the world consider light in much the same way: a spiritual power, the mother of life, ultimate truth, the one universal intelligence, whatever you choose. They all agree, however, that it is the embodiment of all things good: love, joy, wisdom, kindness, bravery and so on. It exists for the spiritual and emotional development of human and sentient kind.

"Moreover, the idea that our souls survive death and move into this light to continue our journey is commonly accepted, even if not directly described in this way. But, there is more to this than is common knowledge amongst most mainstream religions, something that my father's sect understood and had a very real experience of."

Angus got up quietly to put a couple more logs on the fire, and the wine bottle was passed around the table.

"More to the idea of passing into the light at death?" Ed asked.

"Yes. An idea accepted by many people. You know, for sure Ed, of medically recorded accounts of near-death experiences, where the witnesses talk of a light of indescribable beauty, a sublime peace as they went towards it, relatives who had passed before them greeting them from within it." Ed nodded. "But, as in all of life, there is an opposite to this. Broadly speaking, it is not possible for anything to exist without an opposite of some kind. The ancient traditions we have all heard of: Yin and Yang, in-yō, Ouroboros, Yolngu Matha: basically – light and dark.

"But in death, there is not just one and the other. My father explained to me about the layers. At the top, if you like, there is the Light, spirits of the good passing into this. Then there is the layer below this: the Half-light, which those who cannot accept they have died, or those who are unable to leave unsettled amongst the living pass into. They are trapped there until they accept their circumstance and pass up and into the Light. Below this Half-Light is the Dark – as I'm sure you can guess, the souls of intrinsically evil people are imprisoned here, always looking for release into the light above, an escape from their blind existence. In the depths of the Dark, the inhuman entities exist: forces that many people do not even believe exist. As before, different religions call them different things: Satan, Jēh, Rakshasa, Leviathan and so on. But they are all entities that have never been human."

"But other than the Half-Light, isn't that very much the same as what's already accepted by most other religions?" Clara asked.

"Just a handful accept the existence of the Half-light, but none of them, as far as we know, are aware of the final layer – the layer beneath the Dark. This is what my father's religion knew of without doubt, and spent their time, still do as far as I know, fighting to protect human-kind from. Can you imagine trying to convince the rest of the world's established religions that it was real? Although widespread, my father's sect has always been very insular, with little influence. So it made more sense to keep their knowledge to themselves and continue to fight the fight on their own. So far as we know, they have, and continue to be successful in containing the lower layers." Dina refilled her wine glass, and took a few sips.

"So, what's the layer beneath the Dark?" Clara asked.

"It is the antithesis of The Light. In the same way, The Light exists to bring love, joy, compassion, kindness, good. This layer exists to bring destruction, decay, hatred, evil. This is why convincing other religions would be so difficult. They see The Dark itself as responsible for this. It is not. It is just a prison for the souls of wicked people and demons or beings that have never been human if you like. And although the layer beneath The Dark is not alive, it *is* living. You see, there are reasons for the demons above. They are the only way it can spread its influence. It sends up its insidious intentions, and bids them to do its work. But it is forever trying to find ways up, passing strains of itself up through the layers, into the living world. This is where my father's work came in. Wherever this began to happen within my father's boundaries, it was his job to send such strains back beneath The Dark: that is to say – Maintaining The Light."

"How does a strain of this thing get here? To the living?" Jon asked.

"You've heard of the expression, 'beyond the veil', no?"

"Yeah."

"For want of a better articulation, it describes a natural barrier between the living and the dead. There has to be this or there would be no difference between the physical world and the spiritual, and no conduit for souls to pass through to the next stage of their journey. It is this barrier that keeps any occupants of The Dark or strains of the layer beneath from crossing over into this plane.

"In my country, this layer is called 'Zalyshky'. It means 'the dregs'. Everything that is abhorrent, detestable, loathsome, this is Zalyshky: this is its very purpose, its reason for existence. For any part of it to be brought into our world, it must find a gateway. For this, it never stops searching." She looked around the table. "For a gateway to be here on this island, someone created enough tears in the natural barrier for it to push through. Someone on this island created that weakness: held seances, Ouija sessions, something of this kind – and often enough to allow Zalyshky to break through. Smash enough small holes in a door, and something much bigger is going to breach that weakened area from the other side."

There was a long silence as everyone took in the enormity of what Dina was describing. Eventually Ed spoke.

"I dread to ask, but, what ultimately happens when Zal...Zyl – a part of this layer gets through. That hasn't fully happened yet, has it? I have a horrible feeling we've just seen the beginning."

"You are right, Ed," Dina said. "You are witnessing a trail. Zalyshky is following the trail of living essence left behind by whoever punched these holes, so to speak. Remember, it is not living. It is blind. All it can sense is this trace of life energy – precious and irresistible, and so it follows this. It follows wherever it's invitee has been, getting ever closer."

Ed's face darkened. "So, the ultimate result is this invitee getting, what, possessed in some way?"

Dina shook her head. "That would not be so bad. That would be the end of the trail and we could deal with that particular person, no? The danger would be already contained, but Zalyshky wants life. It wants to *be* alive, to become fully sentient so it can bring with it carnage and suffering on an unimaginable scale. It does not want the invitee's body; it wants his life source. As it gets closer to this person, it absorbs what they have left behind – much like the way we leave behind a human scent, we leave behind imprints of our presence for a while wherever we go. This is what it is doing, and leaving in its wake destruction and decay – the rust, the dry rot, the seaweed, the mould, the food – everything rots and dies in its wake, but this is unintentional – it is simply the nature of Zalyshky that causes such phenomena, which, in my view, makes it even more repugnant. However, after some time, its trail wanes as it moves on, much like the animal scent, and so this phenomenon stops."

Jon nodded. "So we know the order this person has been at the locations then – museum, library, beach and the church. That at least gives us a trace line to start with. We need to find the person who's been screwing around with seances or such like as soon as possible, right?"

"If we do not, this person will die," Dina said. When Zalyshky catches up with them, it will simply draw out their very 'being', and then it will be truly alive." She stared at the middle of the table for a second, then back up. "Free to destroy on a scale we cannot comprehend."

"Is there any CCTV covering those places?" Angus asked

"The island has no public coverage, but the library and the museum did. We searched from about fifteen minutes before Frank closed up and the same before Brenda came in, and then surprisingly, a few seconds after that, the footage goes static. He looked back to Dina. "What do we do once we find this person?" Jon asked.

"That's the problem," Dina said, with a heavy sigh. She paused for what seemed like a long time. "I do not know."

"You're kidding me?" Jon said.

"This is as much as my father told me. You must remember, their techniques were highly secretive, not something even a father could tell his daughter. When we moved to the UK, he retired from this work. He was too old to cope with the travelling anymore, and he never spoke of it again.

"Two things, obviously, we need to do: find this person and save them, and send Zalyshky back beneath The Dark. This I know for certain, as I'm sure all of you now do, but I'm sorry." She shrugged her shoulders and looked very matter of fact. "I do not know how."

TWENTY-SEVEN

The clinic was so different when it was empty, such a far cry from the bustling day as pets and owners crowded the reception area, examination rooms were filled with the sounds of so many different animals, the phone always ringing, and the heady smell of disinfectant in the air.

Now, all he could hear was the low hum of the fluorescent lights, and the wash of the waves less than four hundred metres from the entrance. He couldn't remember when he'd been happier in a job. He'd been a veterinary nurse for twelve years now, and had never worked in a practice set virtually on the seafront: nor with such friendly and professional staff. They were all so passionate about the animals, everyone, from Linda the receptionist to the practice owner, Nic Dufour. Ben had a particular respect for Nic, a French vet, who had dedicated much of his spare time to voluntary work with the Worldwide Veterinary Service, before moving to the UK: here, he'd formed EmerVet, a franchise that gave people who struggled financially, access to top-quality animal care. Nic had also happily taken him under his wing, and after just two years under his guidance, Ben was already in a position to begin the first study steps towards becoming a vet himself.

Now, he sat in reception, thinking how much the absence of activity reminded him of an empty theatre – in fact of any building whose sole purpose was accommodating hives of activity when it was empty – it just never seemed quite right. For the next five minutes, he watched the clock on the wall opposite, the countdown to 9pm. The hospital section was empty, which was unusual, no overnight guests, but it meant an early finish for him, and by the time he double-checked the locks on both the drug cabinets and the exam room doors, his shift was over.

He pulled on his coat, and switched off all the lights except one row down the centre of the reception area. But as he turned to the door to go, the room suddenly seemed to dim. He looked up at the light strips – they looked fine – but the room still looked as if someone had draped fine netting across the bulbs. He paused for a moment, then shrugged his shoulders and stepped out into the night, locking the door behind him.

TWENTY-EIGHT

Dina raised her hands, as she saw the crestfallen look on everyone's faces in the kitchen firelight. "I've never had to deal with this myself, but do not worry so quickly. I think my mother will be able to help."

"Not your father?" Jon asked.

"He died eight years."

"So how can your mother help? Did she ever work with your father?"

"No, but she knew what he did, and fully supported him." She shifted in her seat, straightening herself. "My father always took with him a large, brown leather bag when he went away. Never at any other time did I see him with it. And whenever he returned, mother took it from him, and it vanished. I have no idea where she kept it, but I never once saw it in the house. Clearly, it was kept away from me on purpose."

"So you think the tools he used, or the knowledge he had were contained in that bag?" Jon asked.

"Of course," Dina said. "It was too small for clothes and the like, and besides, this he carried in normal luggage. And so I need to speak to my mother and find out where that bag is now."

She got up. "Where is your phone, please, Will?"

Will winced as he pointed to the door of the utility room. "In there, young lady. Please help yourself."

"Does it have hands free?" she asked. "That way everyone can listen, and I don't have to repeat everything."

"Ah, well if you want that, best to use the phone in the dining room."

They all rose, and Will led the way. Once everyone was sat around the oak dining table, Will gestured towards a pile of cloths on a shelf behind him. "Phone's under there, if someone would like to grab it."

Ed was nearest and the cord was long enough to set it down in the middle of the table. Dina drew it over to herself and dialled, punching the key with the 'ear' symbol on it, the line clear through the phone's speaker. It was soon answered by a voice that was elderly, but with a strong, confident tone.

"Hello, Anna Melnyk speaking."

"Zdrastuyter, maty, tse ya," Dina said.

"Dina, moya kokhana, yak ty?" her mother replied.

"Ya duzhe dobre, but English from now on, please, Mother, we have guests listening in."

"Of course. So what is happening? Are you at the university? Are they students?"

"They are friends, Mother, and we need your help."

"Always, my dear. Go on."

"When Father was on his Christian work, he always took the leather bag with him. And you always spirited it away on his return. Do you still have it?"

For a moment, her mother didn't reply. Everyone around the table began looking at each other. This woman could be their last hope, but a second later she spoke.

"Are you in trouble, Dina?" she asked, her voice grave.

"No, no. But I have friends who are. You know I would never ask you if it were not serious. I need to know if Father used the contents of that bag to 'Pidtrymuvaty Svitlo'."

"Bud' laska, ne kazhit' meni, shcho vy namahayetes' maty spravu iz Zalyshkamy samostiyno!" her mother asked, sounding horrified.

"English, please, Mother," Dina said.

"Please do not tell me you are trying to deal with Zalyshky by yourself!"

"I am not. There are good people here with me. Strong people, who understand, and they need to know how to send Zalyshky back down. Somehow a strain of it has broken through, and many lives are at risk. We can't let it gain life – you know that. So where is Father's bag now? Do you still have it?"

"Tell me what has happened, please, Dina," her mother begged.

"We don't have time, Zalyshky is already very close to finding the person who brought it here. Maty - please just trust me – do you still have the bag, and can it help us?"

"Yes, it is still here. Although I do not know what it holds, Dina. My job was to keep it hidden, and when we moved here, your Father retired: he never used it again and it stayed hidden."

"Can you get it for us now?"

"I will, my dear. You must hold on. I will be back in minutes." There was a loud 'clonk' as her mother put the handset down to one side. No one spoke as they waited for her to come back on the line. It was a couple of minutes before they heard the handset being picked up.

"I have it," her mother said.

"Have you opened it?" Dina asked.

"Not yet. It's very light," her mother said, surprise in her voice. "Hang on…" They could hear the squeak of leather, the metallic jingle of buckles, and a moment later she said, "It's empty."

Dina looked bewildered. Everyone else looked horror-struck. "Are you sure?"

There was a rustle, presumably as her mother gave the bag a good rummage. "One moment…" More rustling then, "There is a piece of paper."

"That's it?"

"Yes, my dear. Just this paper."

The frustration in Dina's voice was apparent. "Is there anything written on it, Mother?"

"Wait whilst I get my glasses," her mother said.

Audible sighs could be heard around the table, most of all from Dina as another 'clonk' came from the speaker, but very quickly, she was back. "It has an address on it, nothing else."

"No name or phone number?"

"Just an address. In Sheffield."

Ed looked at Jon. "That's got to be four hours away minimum."

Dina looked around, motioning for a pen and paper. Will pointed to the shelf behind him again, and Ed found a scrap of A4 and a pencil and pushed it over to Dina.

"Ok, read it out to me," Dina said, and took down the address. "Thank you. Now, do not worry, Mother. I must go as time is against us. I'll call you again tomorrow to keep you from worrying."

"Ya lyublyu tebe moya lyuba dochko. Bud'te hranychno oberezhni," her mother said, her voice breaking slightly.

"I will, Maty, I promise. Speak soon. Lyublyu tebe," Dina said.

"I love you too," her mother replied, and Dina hung up gently.

"Sheffield is a long way," Ed said. "You're probably looking at an eight hour round trip. That could be too late."

"Not on a blue light run," Jon said. "Using motorways and A-roads I can cut that in half. If we set off now, we can make the last ferry: at this time of night we'll be there in about two hours."

"But we've no idea who lives there, or if they are even anything to do with Dina's father, or with any of this at all," Clara pointed out. "It could be a huge waste of time, then this thing will be even closer to the invitee and we'll be a man down, two if you and Ed both go."

"We have no choice," Jon said. "At this point in time, this address is the only lead that may give us a way to send this strain back down to its layer. The alternative is to sit here and do nothing. We all know what's going on now, but none of us have a clue how to stop it. What else do you suggest?"

Dina cut in. "I will go with Jon. It may be at this address there is someone I know, or someone my father knew."

"And can I suggest we sit tight until you get back," Ed said. "This thing has already attacked Will – so something no one seems to have considered yet is that, at some at point, this invitee must have been around here. The only good thing about that, is that the strain passed through: presumably to continue tracking them, so this is probably the safest place to be right now. We need to look after ourselves. If we all end up on the business end of this strain, there'll be no one left to stop it. Will, you need to start wracking your brains as to who's been at this house recently that could possibly be the culprit."

Will shook his head. "I've not had a visitor for, what, two weeks now, except for you lot."

"Well they must have been here without your

knowledge. Not necessarily in the house, but maybe the grounds?"

Will shrugged the shoulder of his good arm. "It's possible, I suppose."

Jon interjected. "That sounds a sensible strategy. Let's get going, no point in wasting any more time." He stood up. "We'll try and call you if it's possible when we get there, let you know what's going on." He turned to Angus. "It wouldn't hurt to have another pair of hands either. Can you call Kyle, get him over here?"

"Sure," Angus nodded. All except Will followed Jon and Dina to the front entrance. "Just be careful, Jon," his friend said.

"You know me, Angus, always by the book, and that includes my driving."

"Yeah, I *do* know you, that's why I'm telling you to be careful," Angus opened the door for them, and they stepped out into the night.

"If this goes right, we should get back between 2 and 3am," Jon said and with that, they disappeared into the mist.

Angus closed the door, slid the bolts across the bottom and top, and using the keys Will had left on the hall table, double-locked the mortice.

He turned, looked at Clara and Ed. "I'll give Kyle a call then. I'm sure he'll be thrilled at this time of night."

"Knowing Kyle, I think he'll be well up for it," Clara said with a sideways smile. "And frankly, this is starting to scare the hell out of me. Not something I'd usually admit, so having another person about the place will make me feel better, even if it doesn't really do much."

"I'm with you on that," Ed said. "I'm just hoping to God they find what we need at this address."

"If they don't, then what the hell do we do?" Angus asked.

They all looked at each other for some time, but in the end, no one could find a thing to say.

TWENTY-NINE

After coming off the major roads, which Jon had taken for most of the journey, they had hit country lanes, and the blue light bouncing off of the trees and bushes in silence made it feel strangely surreal in contrast to the screaming two-tones and 140mph of the motorways.

It was around 12:30am when the satnav told them they were in the exact postcode of the address – Broad Acres Stop, Danford, S33 0AX - but so far, there was nothing but fields. They were touching the edge of the Peak District now, the last place they went through, a small hamlet more than six miles or so behind them. Ahead, the road was now straight for as far as the headlights reached, but still no village sign. Jon slowed and turned off the blues. He flicked on full beam and in the distance, the white luminosity of a sign reflected back.

"Could be it," Jon said, and cut his speed again, dropping to 30mph. As they got nearer, they could see that the lane bent ninety degrees to the left, and the sign was slightly set back in a driveway directly opposite the turn.

Dipping his headlights he pulled into the drive to read it: stopping on a bend was not an option. To their surprise, it was a large wooden sign, hung over the entrance to a peculiar-looking building by a small chain at either end, swaying restlessly. Every few seconds, a hollow whistling came from the chains as the wind rushed through them. The fluorescent lettering read: 'Broad Acres Stop'.

"What kind of building is this?" Dina asked. "It's odd."

Jon nodded slowly. "Ah – I see: it's an old railway station. This area is presumably Broad Acres, and this is just the one stop for trains, I imagine: or used to be, hence, Broad Acres *Stop*." He pulled further in and cut the engine. They sat in the pitch night, not a light from anywhere providing respite, the gale whipping around the car. "It doesn't look very occupied."

"I'm thinking the same," Dina said.

"Only one way to find out," Jon said and unbuckled his seat belt. Dina did the same and they both got out. Pulling their collars up against the weather, they jogged across to the entrance. The station was a small red brick building, the disused rails to the rear, now overgrown, disappearing into the night. What had been the ticket office and waiting room to the right, and to the left, two storeys with arched windows in both. Here, the brickwork looked cleaner, the window fittings as if new, and guttering had clearly been replaced not too long ago. The same could not be said for the ticket hall that they stood in front of, it's pointing all but crumbled, paint peeling and flaked, and all the wood fittings looked rotten.

Jon tried the door, it opened with ease and they got inside quickly. Almost all of what must have been the waiting area and ticket office was gutted. The structure was intact, but marks on the floor, torn wood joins, and broken plaster were clear indications that integral furniture and counters had been ripped out. The wall that would have been behind this public area was the strangest: where two doorways once were, there was now brick, but that which would have been the back entrance to the ticket counter was a front door: a common-or-garden, red-painted front door, complete with brass letterbox and knocker.

They looked at each other. "I can't decide whether that's funny or scary," Dina said. "It looks like something out of a child's storybook."

"Yeah, but I'm getting used to bloody odd stuff happening at the moment," Jon said, a wry look on his face. "Whoever owns the place is converting it by the looks of things, but it's seems a backward way of doing it."

"I'm a little worried about the kind of reception we will get, Jon. We don't even know if this place is connected to my father – the paper, it may have just been dropped in the bag by accident."

Jon took out his warrant card. "The magic ticket." He

moved to the front door, Dina following. "Here goes nothing," he said and knocked loudly.

There was no response for a good minute, so Jon tried again, hammering the brass against the door as hard as he could. This time, they heard movement: an interior door, the creak of floorboards, then footsteps.

"Who the hell is it?" a voice behind the door demanded.

"Police," Jon said. "It's nothing to worry about, but we need to speak to you urgently."

"At this time of night, for God's sake?"

"As I said, it's extremely urgent, otherwise we wouldn't be here."

There was a pause, then the sound of locks being undone, and a chain being slid into its housing. The door opened a few inches, and a face appeared, backlit by a hall light. Jon held up his warrant card. "I'm Sergeant Jon Pearce, and this is my colleague who's working forensically with me on the case."

The face peered at the card. "Hmm. Ok, come in, if you really must. Ridiculous hour." The door closed partially, the sound of the chain sliding off, and it was opened fully. The man was in his early forties, wrapped in a black dressing gown, his feet bare. Shaggy, silver-blonde hair framed deep-set eyes, prominent cheekbones and a narrowing jaw. He turned, waving with a tired hand for them to follow and took them along the short hall to a large, modern kitchen with white marble tops, and brushed chrome fittings. An ample breakfast bar sat in the middle, and he motioned to the chairs along each side. "Help yourself," he said. "Coffee?"

"Please," Dina said.

"That would be great, thanks," Jon said. "I'm sorry to call so late, but we needed to speak to you as soon as possible. It might sound odd, but all our investigation came up with was this address but no name, so can I ask who you are?"

The man turned, a look of amusement on his face. "You came here to speak to me, but don't know who I am?"

"We knew we needed to speak to the occupant. I presume this is your place?"

"Yeah," the man said, taking mugs from a cupboard. "I grew up here and when my father died he left it to me." Flicking the kettle switch, he turned back to them. "I'm Alex Reindorp," he said, offering a hand.

Jon shook it. "This is Dina Melnyk," he said.

"Thank you for talking to us, Alex," Dina said, shaking his hand.

Alex looked at her for a moment, then turned back to coffee making. "So what's this all about? How do you think I can help you?"

"We're trying to trace some very rare artefacts that could give us a break in our case. Lives are very much at stake. We think you might be able to help us find them."

Alex came to the breakfast bar with a tray of coffees,

handed them out and sat down with his own. "You're not looking for artefacts, are you?" he said with a smile on his face.

"We are – "Jon began, but the man cut him off.

"You're looking for your father's books, right?" he said, turning his attention to Dina.

Dina studied him, failing to hide her surprise. "I – "

"I know who you must be - you're Artem Melnyk's daughter."

"Yes! How do you know?"

"Considering my own father worked with yours for many years, with your name being Melnyk, it was glaringly obvious."

"Who was your father?" Dina asked.

"He was a priest. Canon Michael Reindorp. He worked with Artem for years. Until I was old enough, he just used to say he was 'good old fashioned back up', but in later years, he brought me into his confidence and trusted me with the knowledge of what he was doing. Dina, you must know about Maintaining The Light?"

"Of course. My father told me much the same as you I imagine, but I think not in such detail."

"What about you, Sergeant? How involved are you with this?" Jon explained as succinctly as possible about the events on the island, but didn't need to go on for long before Alex held up his hand.

"Okay, I get it. I've heard this sort of thing many times from my father. You must both realise how dangerous this is then?"

"Which is why we hope you can help us," Dina said. "We know part of Zalyshky has broken through, we know there is an invitee roaming the island, but that is the extent of our knowledge. We do not know how to stop it."

"I do," Alex said.

"Thank Christ for that," Jon said, the huge relief evident on his face.

"When Artem retired and moved to the UK, he gave his bag to my father for safekeeping. He didn't want the worry of having it in his possession anymore. When my father died two years ago, he passed that responsibly to me. I'm an archivist. I have a passion for ancient documents, but my job covers many different fields, so he knew I understood the importance of the bag contents and that I would guard them well. It contained ancient and rare books and documents, their contents full of powerful – and dangerous – knowledge." He took a sip of coffee. "It's why he kept this place purposely dishevelled. He didn't want to attract any interest. But I was very lucky that my father left me well off. That's why I can now afford to get this place done up on the inside." He took one sip of coffee then stood up. "But keeping it looking ramshackle, more importantly, makes it the last place anyone is going to look for this -." He beckoned them with a hand, and they followed him out of the kitchen. Immediately to the left was a door. Alex opened it, reached in, and tugged at a long chord. The bright light lit up a staircase, and at the bottom, built into the structure of the house itself, was a safe door. It was the length and breadth of a standard house door, but with immense hinges, a keypad set into the wall on the right.

They went down, and before opening the door Alex turned to them. "I have my own private collection – all legal I might add – and they have taken me years to collect. It's like a puzzle: finding different parts of a document, then hunting for another, and another, from all over the world. As much as the safe is to stop anything getting out, it is much more about keeping the outside world protected. There are books and manuscripts in here that are extremely dangerous if put in the wrong hands. I would normally tell anyone I was showing this to that I didn't care if they believed that or not, but you've seen enough for yourself to know I'm speaking the truth." He punched in a combination on the keypad. "Don't touch anything – nothing at all," he said, and the door began to open slowly and smoothly. As it completed its journey, red lights beyond fluttered on automatically, and a room, the ground area of the entire building, stretched out before them. Shelves ceiling-high ran the length of the room, with a gap in between each, just wide enough for a person to walk down.

Alex led the way in. "Red light causes less damage to documents," he said, "not that I usually have them out for any length of time. But it's better to be cautious when preserving this kind of material." He took them to the start of a shelf a few feet along, and from a dispenser

226

on the end of it, tugged out a pair of latex-free gloves and pulled them on. "If you stay there a moment," he said and started walking along the gaps, past volumes of books, papers, manuscripts, all carefully labelled. It wasn't long before they saw him carefully extract a book about A4 size and return.

"This," he said, "is the genuine translation of 'Light On The Path'. It's one of three treatises from a book written by Helena Petrovna Blavatsky called The Voice of Silence. She was a Russian occultist and philosopher from the late nineteenth century. She was regarded by many as a charlatan, but often those critics were people who saw her as dangerous because she undermined their religious beliefs with cogent argument and theories ahead of her time, but she also had a huge following – those who already understood her concepts, had their own very real experiences of them, knew how important her work was, and how much power was contained within her writings. She travelled the world extensively for many years, and she wrote down her gathered knowledge from such excursions in many books, most of which are now lost. There are only four or five that anyone knows of."

They had both expected something a little more grandiose, a huge, black leather-bound monstrosity of some kind perhaps – but in a way, the innocuous appearance of the book seemed to make it all the more awe-inspiring.

"The most famous of her writings, 'The Book of

Golden Precepts' is thought to be her translation of a sacred book she discovered on her travels in the East. But it's not. In truth, it's a translation from many different sacred texts she came across, and the public version of this book contains a completely different translation. As far as we know, around ten copies of her original translations exist, containing those three treatises. This is one of them, and a small part of it lays out in true detail exactly how to send the likes of Zalyshky back to the level in which it belongs.

"Obviously, I can't let you take this away. I'll copy the pages you need, but you have to keep them on you at all times – they must never leave your person."

"I give you my word," Dina said.

"And you truly understand how dangerous this material is?"

"Of course."

"Good. The pages describe exactly what you have to do – how to set things up, who needs to be present, who does what and so on. Follow it to the letter. Do not deviate, do not repeat anything, okay?"

"Okay."

"I trust you, as a Melnyk, as my father trusted yours."

"Thank you. And thank you for helping us," Dina said.

"Knowing what you're facing it was never a question," Alex said. "Hang on here and I'll run off the copies you need." He walked along the rows of shelves and disappeared round the very last one. They heard the clunking of a photocopier and a minute later he was back.

He'd put them in a plain white folder, and held a pen in his other hand. "Don't study them now. You need a clear head, not jiggling about in a car seat at some ludicrous time in the morning on a motorway, okay?" he said and handed them to Dina. "And whatever happens, make absolutely sure you burn them afterwards. Nothing less – no shredder, no scissors. Burn them. Here's my number," he said writing on the folder. "Call me when you've done so, and I can put my mind at rest." He looked at them both. "Now get on your way, don't waste any time."

"What actually happens when we do this?" Jon said nodding at the folder.

"I haven't a clue. I've never done it. I just know those pages tell you how. Let me know – I'd be extremely interested."

"Well, if I don't die during the process, I'll give you a call," Jon said with a dry smile.

"Stick to those pages, and you'll be fine," Alex said.

"We will, I can assure you," Dina said.

Alex led the way back up the stairs, the safe door closing automatically behind them, and took them to the front door.

"Thank you for this, Alex," Jon said shaking his hand. "You could well have saved lives."

"Very glad I was able to help," Alex said. He took Dina's hand. "It was special to have met you, Dina.

Your father was an incredible man."

"Thank you. And the same for me," she said.

"Safe journey back."

As they crossed the ticket office, the wind rattling the old windows and shaking the guttering, Alex called out to them one last time.

"But just bear in mind – if you screw this up – if you get this wrong – you risk inviting up hell itself."

THIRTY

Nic Dufour raised arms as if praising God but the motion was far from celebratory. "What the hell is all of this, Jon?" His mild French accent was more pronounced than usual.

Every animal cage, every medical instrument, every inch of anything metal, was caked in rust. All the drugs had either turned to some weird kind of gloop, or solidified, the food in the kitchen fridge had begun to rot, and doorframes, desktops and other wooden fittings had begun to split and scar with dry rot.

"Uh...I really don't know, Nic," Jon lied. "Absolutely bizarre, I must say." He still felt tired despite five hours sleep. They'd arrived back from Broad Acres at around 3am, and he'd gone straight to bed. But it had only felt like seconds later when his radio had kicked into life, summoning him to EmerVets.

"I didn't know who else to call. I'm probably wasting your time, but, well..." he said and shrugged his shoulders.

"I'll get Jason to come over and run some tests. It

could be something atmospheric, something carried in from off-shore."

"I have no idea, but it means I'll not be able to open for some time. Perhaps I could relocate for non-operative patients," he said. "I'll have to see what I can do. Thankfully, we had no hospital cases last night. I checked with Ben: he left at 9pm, and he says everything was normal."

Thank Christ for that, Jon thought, extremely relieved to hear it. At least they knew no one was wandering about injured, or worse. "This will seem an odd question, Nic, but has anybody seen anything unusual here in the last couple of days, or has anything odd happened – apart from this, of course?"

The vet sat himself down on a chair, thinking. "How odd, Jon? There are strange little things that happen with animals, and their owners even. Always stories to tell, working here, but nothing I would term as odd, certainly not on this scale." He indicated the room with a roll of his eyes.

"Well, something that you noticed particularly, something out of the every day."

"In that case, the only thing I can recall is Birdie running off like he did."

"Birdie?"

"Lucas Crane. He's a young lad who comes in once a week and helps out as a volunteer. He loves it. Been coming for, oh, I would say, a year almost."

"I know of Lucas," Jon said, "but I've never had

dealings with him. Didn't know he got called, 'Birdie'."

"He's a nice lad, but quiet. A little withdrawn, I would say, but a hard worker."

"So what happened with him?"

"Yesterday afternoon it was quiet. So, we were taking a break – myself, Ben, Monica, and Linda. Lucas was sweeping the front of reception, and I was telling them about William Brooksbank's injury. I have a friend who works in A&E, and yes, I know I shouldn't have been discussing it. What can I say – I'm French, I like gossip."

"The Italian's are worse, Nic," Jon said with a smile.

"Anyway, I was saying how lucky he was not to have damaged anything major, but that he wouldn't be painting for a while. Linda was then telling me how much his painting meant to him, and just like that – whoosh – Lucas is gone. He runs through the surgery, out of the back doors and that's that."

Jon raised his eyebrows. "And you think it was to do with what you were talking about?"

"Definitely – he stopped sweeping for a few moments, listening to our conversation, and when I started to talk about William, that was when he was off." Nic paused, then said, "Do you think Lucas had anything to do with this? I don't see how that's at all possible."

"No, no. Of course not. But no other strange occurrences?"

"That's the only thing I would say was out of the

normal at all, Jon."

"Okay," Jon said. "Well, as promised, I'll get Jason over here as soon as possible, see what we can come up with."

Nic shrugged again. "Thank you, I appreciate that, but I think there is not much he will discover. This is the strangest thing I think I've ever seen."

"We can only try. Jason has some good contacts in other fields, so maybe they can help."

"That would be good," Nic said. "I hope so."

"I'll speak to you once we have any results," Jon said heading for the door. "Give me a shout if you remember anything else unusual," he said, and went out, still thanking God on high that last night, the place had been empty.

THIRTY-ONE

As soon as he'd left the vets, Jon had radioed the nick to see if they had anything on Lucas Crane. Other than Jason knowing him to be a loner, and in his own words 'a right bloody weirdo', there was nothing – no information reports, no driver stops, not even a parking ticket: his home address wasn't on the electoral roll, either. A great start, Jon thought.

He needed to tell everyone about Lucas, so headed back to Will's place. There he found everyone gathered in the kitchen, as was becoming the norm, including Kyle now. It was the warmest room for a start, the ample fire always burning, and the wine was within easy reach, either in the fridge or from the rack next to it.

Dina had brought everyone up to speed regarding Alex Reindorp and the documents, and although they were in Russian - their language shared common attributes but there were differences in some of their alphabet, and some words had completely different meanings – she'd managed to read it all.

"Birdie," Will exclaimed when Jon had told him

about the vets.

"Why Birdie?" Jon said.

"Crane. It's a bird," Kyle said smirking. "Good job they never made you a detective."

Jon gave him a sarcastic smile. "Up yours, mate," he said, "and thanks for coming, by the way. I appreciate it." He turned back to Will. "So you know Lucas?"

"Sort of. Bit of an oddball. In his early twenties I suppose, a loner. He was born on the island – his mother used to restore silverware and I used her services over the years. She died last year and left her cottage to the boy, but he rarely spends any time there from what I can tell. He prefers to sleep outside – God only knows why. He was up in the copse at the back of my place the night before last."

"So, we can definitely place him here, and at the vets – I know you checked the CCTV, Jon, but we need to look much further back. If we find footage of this guy at both places then it goes beyond coincidence. It doesn't matter if we can't place him with Gibson or at the church."

"I'll get Jason to do that straight away," Jon said.

"What about checking the camera to see if Lucas is one of Gibson's recent victims?" Clara asked.

"We can't," Jon said, "it's at the lab on the mainland, but I think it's unlikely. Gibson went for those who couldn't fight back. I know Lucas isn't exactly Bruce Willis, but he'd be able to fend off Gibson in a situation like that."

"And there's no CCTV at or around the church?" Ed asked.

Jon shook his head. "'Fraid not. But as you say, Ed, it already seems way too much of a coincidence that he was at the vet's, and here two nights ago and both places get hit."

"If I hadn't heard this from the likes of you, Jon, and Will, I'd have thought it was a load of old horse shit," Kyle said. "But I've seen some weird stuff in my time, especially when I was in South America, so if you say this stuff is going on, then as far as I'm concerned it's going on, but I'm wondering how I can help?"

"You know the island better than anyone – all the good hiding places, and so on."

"What are you saying?" Kyle said feigning hurt.

"Yeah, yeah. You know I'm right, and if we get no luck at Lucas's home address, we'll need you to help start tracking him down. We need to get to him as fast as possible – before that bloody 'thing' does."

Kyle looked at Jon. "And how persuasive are we supposed to be if we find him and he doesn't want to join in the fun?"

"Do whatever you have to," Jon said, setting off a silence in the room.

Eventually, Kyle said, "Are you sure? You're a straight-up bloke, Jon, you do things right. If he really doesn't play ball, he may get hurt if we have to bring him in forcibly."

"I know. I understand the significance of what I'm

saying, but there's so much more at risk than Lucas – I don't want any harm coming to him - that goes without saying - but if it happens in order to get him in, then so be it. A necessary evil."

"So, who do you want to do what, Jon?" Angus asked.

"Does he drive, Will?" Jon asked. Will shook his head. "Then we need to get to Lucas's home first – obvious port of call. If he's not there, I suggest we split into three pairs and take a section of the island each. From what Nic was telling me of his reaction at the vets, he's frightened. So he's not exactly going to be strolling along the seafront or through open fields. That doesn't leave a huge number of places he can be hiding, which makes our job a bit easier." He brought out a series of small pictures from his back pocket. "Nic copied these for me – it's Lucas's photo from the volunteer notice board." He passed them out. "If Ed goes with Dina, Kyle with Clara, and Angus, if you can take the Land Rover on your own." He fished his car keys from his pocket and worked them around in his hand for a moment. "I'll be back in a moment," he said and disappeared out of the door. Some five minutes later, he returned, a large canvas bag in his hand. He put it down carefully on the kitchen table.

"I hope I'm doing the right thing – it goes against everything in my book, but I feel we have no choice." He unzipped the bag and pulled it open. He took out three handheld tasers, three canisters of CS spray, and three pairs of quick-cuffs. He gave the two pairs and Angus one of each. He then took out five radios and passed them out.

"I'll show you how to use these. It's very simple. But please be aware, what I'm doing is totally illegal. I'm handing over what are classed as firearms under UK law to untrained civilians. This must never go any further than us." He looked at each of their faces in turn, every one of them resolutely serious.

"Please only use them if you have no other choice. The hard fact is, we need to get him in – and as fast as possible."

THIRTY-TWO

It was difficult to distinguish where the gun-grey sky ended, and the sea began. The offshore wind was bitterly cold and came in great, undulating gusts, and the beach below the cemetery was certainly no host to any surfers now.

Before starting their search, Ed and Dina had been tasked to briefly see if they could find anything at all at the Gibson scene that would point to Lucas having been there. They'd started at the bottom of the sand-shelf, found nothing, so had followed the path to the far left that took them up onto the top and amongst the graves.

"I'll start with the path to the woods," Ed said. "You okay to check out the first lot of headstones?"

"Of course," Dina said. "I'll keep my eyes open for severed chicken heads and gris-gris bags."

"Oh, how the Comedy Store beckons," Ed said, and began slowly walking along the path between the thicket. He wasn't really sure what he was looking for, just anything that they might be able to connect to Lucas, he supposed, but he wanted to spend as little time here as possible: finding the lad was more important than anything, and frankly, whether he'd been here or not, was surely now irrelevant. Jason had called in before they all left Will's to confirm that Lucas had been caught on CCTV both at the museum and the library, a good five hours before the events took place. That was all the further confirmation they needed. They'd spend ten or fifteen minutes here, he'd decided, and then begin their search of the area they'd been designated. Neither of them knew the island, so now Jon had given them obvious landmarks to look out for, they had a rough idea how far to go in any one direction.

As he moved along, head down, eyes peeled, his hand moved to the quick-cuffs and CS spray in his coat pocket. He hoped he wouldn't have to use them, but under the circumstances, he'd have no problem doing so if need be. Dina had insisted on having the baton, and with an enthusiasm he found, not shocking as such, just a bit unnecessary. But then again, she'd always been a strong woman in all senses since he'd known her: krav maga classes, off-roading, hill running, fencing and even free climbing. So his surprise was, in hindsight, rather ill-placed.

He was wondering how far along the path to go, when a shout from Dina jolted him from his thoughts.

"I've found something." He turned to see her now, forty feet from him, crouched amongst the graves, one hand in the air and beckoning him. He hurried over and as he got to her, she was standing and he followed her finger that pointed to the large headstone a few feet in front of her. "I've been studying this field nearly all my life," she said, "and I've never seen anything like this before."

"I have," Ed said, beaming. "Makes a change for me to be telling you something."

"Enjoy it," Dina said, trying to keep a straight face, "it will be many years before this happens again,"

On the stone before them, a large symbol was drawn in chalk: a solid circle, and inside this, by an inch, another circle in dashed lines, then again, an inch inside, another solid circle. At the two o'clock position on the outer circle was a simple, triangular arrow, and directly underneath this against the inner one, the number five. Inside the circle itself were drawn four Celtic single spiral knots at the north, east south and west positions, and lastly, at the bottom of the symbol, a series of runes that ran half the circumference.

"What does it mean?" Dina asked. "I've seen the spiral knot many times, but they are not right. Look here." She pointed to the out thread of each knot that should have simply run into the next – one continuous line – but it ended before the next spiral was drawn.

"You know the spiral knot represents the journey from physical life to spiritual life, the constant circle of creation, right?"

"I do."

"These knots have no continuation. They finish, as you can see. They represent a journey from the physical world to the spiritual world, but that ends there, with no hope of rebirth or return."

Dina shook her head. "This is not something I have ever come across before."

"I've only ever seen it once myself. It was on a demonic possession case. The symbol is a gateway, drawn to trap a demon or evil spirit and return it to the spirit world for good." He indicated to the arrow. "This points in the direction of where the demon was originally summoned, and the number underneath, the distance as the crow flies. It's a simple as that. The demon is said to be unable to resist the calling of the rune spell, and enters the circle: but the gateway then takes it straight back to its place of summoning and casts it back down for all time." He ran his finger over parts of the chalk. "This is recent too. The weather hasn't had time to wash much away."

"But why not just draw the symbol at the place of origin?" Dina asked.

"Fear. If a powerful demon had been summoned, no one would want to be near the summoning point. They would prefer to hope the magic worked and that the demon would be unable to resist the gateway symbol, and get rid of it that way. A kind of remote control, I suppose." He gave a short smile. "Ahead of their time, these Celts, you know."

"It's far too coincidental not to be Lucas. He comes here, frightened maybe? Knows he's conjured up something hideous, and tries to send it back. And surprise, surprise, Gibson, the next person along, gets caught in the strain's wake and eaten by the sand-shelf."

"So this is good for us, yes? This tells us that five miles from here, in the direction of the arrow, is the place that this all began."

"Exactly."

"And the pages from Alex tell us the ritual must be carried out at the location of origin."

"Bonus points for us, I think," Ed said. "Right, we need to let Jon know what we've found, and buy a map, asap."

"I need, also, to find the articles for the ritual according to the instructions," Dina said.

"What kind of articles?"

Dina took the folded pages from her inside coat pocket, holding on to them tightly against the wind. She showed him the page that listed the four items. "Two of those won't be a problem," he said, then pointed to the last two items. "But where in the hell we find the this from, I've no idea. If we were on the mainland it might be a bit easier, but here? And the last item - pretty gross, and I doubt, very easy."

"I am thinking this too, Jon," Dina said.

"Let's get to the town - we can wrack our brains on the way," Ed said, and they began making their way quickly back to the beach car park.

THIRTY-THREE

Jon had been ten minutes away from Lucas Crane's home address when Ed had come through on the radio, asking him to meet them urgently: they might have an idea where Lucas could be hiding. So he'd spun around, hit the blues, and arrived at the seafront three minutes later. They were waiting for him in 'The Pie Chart', the island's only bakery-café.

"Please tell me you're not taking a coffee break?" Jon said, half-seriously, as he approached, came in, the bell above the door tingling.

"We bought the map from the newsagent next door, but we then needed a decent table: look at this," Ed said, the joke going straight over his head. On the table was spread a small scale map of the island, a pencil tied to a piece of string to one side of it. "We found a Celtic gateway symbol recently drawn on one of the headstones, right where Gibson had been that day."

"What's it for?" Jon asked.

"It supposed to create a gateway to trap an unwanted spirit that has been summoned. The way it's drawn indicates exactly where the original point of the summoning took place – whether that was a séance, Ouija board, demonic calling, whatever." He indicated the cemetery on the map. "The headstone was about twenty feet from the edge of the sand-shelf, and thirty-foot from where it drops down to meet the beach. So, about here." He picked up the pencil and marked the spot. "There was an arrow on the symbol which is supposed to point towards the place the summoning happened, but we don't know if that should be read as from above, or in front of the gravestone." He straightened the piece of string and held the end of it on the pencil mark. "What we do know from the symbol, is that it's a five-mile radius of this point, which this length of string I've cut to."

"Looking for any buildings cross that radius, right?"

"Exactly," Ed said, drawing a circle. "Even before you arrived, we could see straight away – there was no other building anywhere near that radius." He completed the circle and put the pen down. Jon looked at the map, and only one structure intersected the circle – Long Mire Rectory.

"This is where it all began," Dina said. "And this is where we must set everything up ready to begin the ritual."

"And maybe Lucas is hiding there. If the Celtic gateway didn't work, he might try doing something similar but at the point of origin, even if he's scared."

"That's excellent," Jon said. "Let's err on the side of

caution though. I'll still hit Lucas's home address. You guys get to the rectory and start preparing things. Be a bit clever, though, in case he's already there. We don't want him on the run again. Let me know as soon as you arrive."

"Have your wits about you," Ed said, as Jon made for the door.

"You too," he said and closed it behind him.

Will had given him good directions to Lucas's house, along with a description of the outside as it was, in his words, 'in the middle of bloody nowhere.' With the blues on again, he was racing down what he hoped was the correct country lane within less than twelve minutes. Soon, a right turn on to a mud track would show itself if he had things right. Every second it didn't appear, his heart raced faster. The trees were high on either side, cutting back what poor light there was from the clouded sky. He put his headlights on, slowed a little, and caught sight of the turn as the road bent to the left.

It was only wide enough for one car, deep mud, grass high along the centre, dense woodland on either side, darkening his way even more. He cut the blues, but went to full beam: the last thing he needed was to get stuck. Carefully he made his way along, the car bumping and tipping over the uneven ground, making what must have been a half-mile journey seem like ten. The track ended with a grass clearing, and he rolled slowly into it, and cut the engine. On the other side was the single-storey cottage. It was in a poor state of repair: the thatch was almost bare in places, the guttering had collapsed, two small windows were broken, and half of its dull pink paint had flaked away. The cramped front garden was severely overgrown, and the path to the front door still crowded with enough weeds and foliage to suggest it was only rarely used.

He opened the car door quietly and got out. Unclipping its holster button, he took out his CS spray, shook it, and flipped the lid. Too often officers had been caught off guard using CS spray that had sat on their belt for months, allowing much of the active component to settle at the bottom.

He searched the windows for any sign of life, but they were so grubby, the chances of seeing anything through them was remote anyway. CS spray held at his side, he approached the front door, stepping softly, trying not to disturb too much of the foliage. He placed his ear against it, listened intently, but there was only silence. In this quiet, out here, miles from anywhere, even the sound of the sea had vanished.

He took hold of the latch handle, and to his surprise, it lifted. He paused to see if the sound might have disturbed any occupant. Again, there was nothing. Pushing it open slowly, he kept to one side to ensure he wasn't backlit like a sitting duck. The pungent smell of burnt fat, body odour and damp air hit him at once. He peered into the dark interior, waited for his eyes to adjust. A short hall was before him, a door immediately to the left and right. At the end, what looked like the entrance to a kitchen, but with no door.

He stepped inside, took hold of the left door handle, and turned it. He pushed it open, ready with the spray. The door creaked plaintively, opening into a bedroom, but that was all. In the centre against the back wall was a double bed frame – and even in the dim, Jon could see it was smothered in layers of rust. He immediately looked back at the interior of the front door, down at the wooden door handles, the skirting board and saw the scars of dry rot. The smell of abandonment had disguised any odour from the rust, but now his eyes were used to the gloom, he could see it everywhere, covering anything metal in the place. The rest of the room had no other furniture, and the curtains were still closed.

He moved back into the hall and along to the doorway at the end. Keeping to one side, he looked in. It was a kitchen-diner. And it stank. The putrid scent of decaying food pervaded the air like a living thing: clearly, the room hadn't been used in months, and every scrap of already perished organic matter that was left over, was now made a hundred times worse by the effect of Zalyshky passing throughout. As a police officer he'd come across some of the worst smells a human could, but there was something especially puke-making about the smells this entity left behind. It was only professional pride that had stopped him dry heaving several times recently.

He moved back along the hall and opened the room

on the left, still ready to deal with anyone inside. Although no such person was there, there was certainly plenty to see. It was another bedroom, again, the rust and dry rot rampant throughout. But it had recently been occupied – and left in a hurry by the looks of it. Clothes were strewn across the floor and hanging out of drawers from the one chest of drawers in the room. What looked like a bizarre collection of jewellery and nick-nacks was strewn across the top of it, and scattered across the floor around it.

He moved to the tall bookshelf opposite, scanned some of the titles. None of them meant much to him, but it was obvious they were of an occult nature, as were the posters around the walls. Then he spotted the local papers on the floor, one on a chair next to them, pages turned to the respective stories of Frank's 'accident', the fire at the library and the verger's heart attack. This along with the obvious and hurried exit told Jon this boy was running scared, unlikely to be here at all, but experience had taught him never to take anything for granted. He'd lost two friends who had: the first to an eight-year-old burglar who had a machete hidden down his trouser leg, and the second to an over-friendly druggy who had carefully placed needles along the cushion line of his sofa and offered him a seat whilst asking his preference for coffee or tea.

About to turn and leave, his eye caught something lying on top of the paper on the chair, something that at first, in the gloom, had just looked like part of the newspaper, but he could see now that it was a separate piece of paper. He went over, picked it up, and his stomach flipped over.

He dashed out to the car, rammed the keys home, and hit the blues. Slamming the unmarked into first, mud kicked up violently as he sped out of the clearing and down the narrow lane, this time, no concern for the bumps and potholes, and as he fishtailed on to the main road, he grabbed at his radio and thumbed the 'urgent assistance' button.

THIRTY-FOUR

Kyle was aware Clara thought she knew the island pretty well, but an hour in the car with him and that assumption was out of the window. He'd shown her hidden lanes, unknown lakes, several cottage ruins, two abandoned mining buildings and roads she never even knew existed.

"This is extraordinary," she said, as they cut along one of the wider lanes she'd never seen before.

"Glad you like the more uninterrupted parts of the island," Kyle said, "but keep your eyes peeled. We need to spot this lad."

Clara folded over a small part of the photo Jon had given them and tucked it in the gap between the stereo and the dash, so that they could both see it. "Is that better?" she asked.

"Much," Kyle said. "Weird looking nipper, isn't he?" The photo showed a male in his late teens, a pale face, narrow nose, and thin lips partially hidden by lank, shoulder-length hair cut in a curtain style. His eyes were such a dark brown, they were almost black, accentuated by his bland complexion. They reminded Kyle of a stargazer fish he'd once seen on a school trip to a sea life centre – eyes devoid of much intelligence, and that was it.

"Just be ready if we see him – we'll need to try and get his attention without spooking him."

"I'm ready," Clara said, tapping the taser in her coat pocket.

Kyle frowned. "I'm not sure anyone should be that jolly about packing a taser," he said.

"I know this is serious, but you can't tell me you don't find it exciting?" Clara said. But before he could answer the radio, let out a two-second bleep as the urgent assistance button Jon had pressed the other end created an open channel, so no one could cut in.

"I've just found a ferry ticket reservation slip at Lucas's home address. He's going to try and get off the island. We can't let that happen. Kyle and Clara, can you start making your way to the terminal – I'll do the same. I've still got two Specials down there, so that should give us an advantage. Angus, head to Long Mire Rectory. Ed and Dina discovered it's where this all began. They'll explain more when you get there."

"All received," Kyle said, heard Angus do the same.

"We're heading in that direction already, aren't we?" Clara said.

"Yeah," Kyle said, suddenly breaking, and throwing the car into reverse. Within two turns, they were facing the opposite way and flying along at sixty.

"What are you doing?" Clara said, her voice suddenly strained.

"If I were trying to get off the island without being seen, I certainly wouldn't be taking any main routes. From Will's description of where Lucas lives, it's out near Trayper's Forest. It's a dense stretch of woodland that covers most of the uninhabited countryside to the north of The Borrow. Most people don't know the area very well, but guess what?"

"You do," Clara said.

"Full marks," Kyle said. "There's a path that cuts straight through it, brings you down through the grassland behind the golf course, and then into the town via the back streets. You end up less than half a mile from the ferry terminal." He looked at Clara and smiled. "That's the way I'd be going."

They turned at the next left, so he gunned the engine and dropped a gear, the road rising steeply, now more gravel and mud than tarmac. They continued to climb, the hill maintain its forty-five-degree angle, and it was a good ten minutes before it started to level out as the dense woodland of Trayper's Forest began to close in around them.

Kyle turned the headlights on, the afternoon cloud stealing any chance of decent visibility, especially under the dense treetops. Then without warning, he suddenly turned hard right, over the edge of the road, and Clara yelled out.

"Christ, Kyle, what the hell are you doing?"

"Just hold on," he said, as they immediately hit a track in the trees so narrow they couldn't possibly get through. But as Clara braced her hands against the dashboard, ready for the impact, the dense branches at windscreen height slapped and sprung off the car, whilst below, the path cleared of foliage, allowing them unobstructed passage. It was a clever illusion, and anyone looking at the start of the track would be convinced that it was unpassable.

"So who thought of this, dare I ask?" Clara said, relaxing and letting her hands drop back on to her lap.

"This has been here long before my time," Kyle said. "I certainly won't have been the first to use it for, less salubrious reasons, shall we say. But I'd have to admit to being one of those few on the island who have helped keep it running this way."

"You do surprise me," Clara said.

"Give it a hundred feet and it'll open up," Kyle said, and it did. The greenery suddenly fell away, as if some kind of theatre set had been pulled aside to reveal the next scene. The trees were still closely packed on either side, but the track itself now cut cleanly through the forest. Their engine sound suddenly seemed muted, and Clara wound down the window. The forest floor, smothered in leaves and pine needles dampened every sound, making their progression feel otherworldly and strangely detached.

Kyle slowed the car. "It might be tricky if we see him. He'll know very few people are aware of this track, and if I was on the run and heard a car coming along here, I'd be well out of the way before it got near me."

"Let's hope he's a bit thick then, shall we?" Clara said. "I mean, the idiot has caused all of this in the first place, and that doesn't strike me as the actions of someone who know what they're doing."

"Yeah. The guy obviously knows a bit about all this spooky shit, but doesn't mean to say he's any good at it. Quite the opposite I'd say from what you've all told me."

"So, do you think he'd be just traipsing along like that?" Clara said slowly, raising a pointed finger to the windscreen.

"You're bloody kidding me," Kyle said, peering out.

Just coming in to view through the gloom of the trees was the outline of a person, some kind of bag on their back. Kyle slowed to a crawl and cut to his sidelights, but it was enough to see that it was a wiry male, with lank brown hair, dressed in a fleece, cargo trousers and walking boots.

Kyle glanced at the photo on the dash. "Hard to tell from behind," he said.

"Oh, come on Kyle," Clara said. "You just told me hardly anyone knows about this track, and you'd be on it if you were getting out of here in a hurry. It's not going to be some biology student out on a study ramble, is it?"

"Ok, ok, you're right. It's got to be him." He touched the accelerator lightly, but it was too late. The male's head turned suddenly, the car lights caught the look of fear on Lucas Crane's face, and he was into a run.

"Shit," Kyle spat, and floored the pedal, the mix of leaves and pine needles at first providing no grip. The front wheels span for a second, the mulch flew up and then the tyres bit, sending the car flying forward. Kyle fought to keep it in a straight line but oversteered. The back end swung around violently, sending mud high into the air, the engine squealing. He threw the steering wheel back the other way, but too fast, and the tyres lost grip again, straining against the natural momentum of the car, and the rear wing smashed into the trees in an explosion of metal and glass, throwing Clara's head against her window. She shook her head, bringing her hand to her temple.

"Christ alive! Are you ok?"

"I think so." She took her hand away and looked at it. "No blood," she said. "But things are spinning a bit."

"Stay here," Kyle said. "Don't move." He pushed the radio into her hand. "Tell the others what's happened. I'm going after Lucas. We can't lose him now."

He threw off his seatbelt, and bolted from the car, slamming the door behind him. He knew he was fast, but he just hoped Lucas had stayed on the path. If the lad veered off without him seeing, it could be almost impossible finding him in such dense forest. As he covered the first hundred yards, he caught sight of Lucas, still running along the track, clearly hampered by the rucksack and walking boots.

Kyle pushed himself into the next gear, his legs like

steam pistons, arms slicing the air. But just as he was within thirty feet of him, Lucas suddenly veered right, and disappeared into the trees.

Kyle was close enough to hear him as he crashed through the woods, so he cut straight into the trees. The ground began to slope as he gained on the lad, becoming muddy. With the wet, uneven ground, Lucas's footwear was now a help, not a hindrance. The pace had slowed but Kyle couldn't get a decent grip underfoot to take advantage of it. He kept having to look down to negotiate his way, and each time he looked up, Lucas's was that bit farther away, and was now began working his way down the slope, as well as along.

In the next fifty feet, the rake quickly became so acute that Kyle found himself with his left arm out, pushing away from the ground, moving foot over foot just to stay upright, and the next time he looked up, Lucas was gone.

He stopped for a second and listened. He could still hear undergrowth being trampled, but far down to his right now. A second later the sound had gone. It didn't fade, it just stopped. So, Kyle thought, either the lad was worn out, or he had decided to hide. Either way, it gave him the chance to make up ground.

He peered down through the trees directly to his right and could just make out the bottom of the incline, so instead of moving forward, he carefully made his way down, keeping his feet as much as possible on mud and clear of obvious branches and debris. His progress was quiet enough that he would still hear if Lucas set off again, but there was no indication of such. A couple of minutes later he reached the bottom of the slope. It flattened out into a wide, solid earth path, and beyond this, a small riverbed. He listened again, but the only sound was the water flowing gently by.

The path made quiet advancement fairly easy, and as much as he could, he stuck to the tree-line, trying to keep his profile low. Forty feet ahead, the path widened again as the river curved to the right, and the ruins of several brick buildings rose from it. Old miner's cottages probably, Kyle thought. He'd shown Clara the same earlier, further north. And this had to be the place Lucas was hiding.

Instead of continuing to follow the path, Kyle pulled himself up on to the foot of the slope, tucking in amongst the trees again, gaining some high ground above the ruins as he drew parallel to them. He half crouched, peering through branches, scanning the brick remains for any sign of the lad. Nothing from this angle, so he carefully moved a little further along and took another look. Again, he saw no sign of him, but there were so many nooks and corners he could be tucked away in it was almost a fruitless exercise.

Suddenly there was a flutter of birds ahead and to his left, and he ducked slightly, scanning the ruins – and saw him. The wiry figure was running again, flashing in and out of view in between the brickwork remains.

Kyle was on his feet, barrelling through the branches

and out on to the path. He had the advantage back now the ground was pretty much level again, and vaulting two low-level walls, once again he found himself directly behind Lucas. He drove himself forward, could see that Lucas was slowing, but wasn't about to give him an inch. A few seconds and he was three feet away, and with a final, colossal burst of energy, he launched himself forward into the air, clamping his arms around the lad's waist, slamming him to the ground.

Lucas let out an involuntary gasp as the air in his lungs was forced out, and lay motionless, eyes closed. Kyle stood up, rummaging for the quick-cuffs in his rear jeans pocket, but he stopped midway, looking down at the lad.

"Shit. Are you okay?" He pushed Lucas's foot several times with his own. "Lucas?" He pushed again, a bit harder. "Lucas?" There was no reaction. "Oh, great. I've killed the idiot." He watched his chest and let out a big sigh when he saw it rise and fall a moment later. There was no way he could carry him back up the steep incline, so he had no choice but to wait until he came round. He backed up to a bit of collapsed wall, and leant against it, folding his arms. Around him, the forest had become decidedly darker, and colder for that matter. He pulled his jacket collar up around his neck and watched Lucas to ensure he didn't suddenly stop breathing.

It was a good five minutes before he began to stir, legs sliding slowly against each other first, followed shortly by agitated arm movement. Then he started mumbling, a sure sign he would soon regain consciousness. Kyle pushed himself up from the wall and took out the quick-cuffs. He knelt down and fixed the first cuff to Lucas's left arm, just as the lad turned his head and half-opened his eyes.

"Don't worry, Lucas, I'm not going to hurt you. You may not believe it but I'm here to help you," Kyle said.

Lucas looked as if he was trying to focus his eyes, his head lolling a little. He mumbled again, but with a tone of urgency.

Kyle reached over and took hold of Lucas's right arm. "You're okay. I'm going to take you to Jon Pearce, the copper. He's going to help you out, alright?"

"Listen, this is important," Lucas said, his voice a whisper. He mumbled again, and Kyle brought his face closer.

"Say that again, lad."

Another mumble.

Kyle brought his ear closer to lad's mouth –

- and a piercing lance of pain shot through his head as Lucas drove his knee into his temple. He collapsed sideways, his entire body limp as Lucas scrambled to his feet and stood over him. Although the agony in his skull had misted his vision, Kyle could just make out the face of person in the unbreakable grip of unadulterated terror. Then, for a second, his sight flashed white and coloured flecks darted in front of him, and he could hear the sound of something being dragged across the ground. After a few more dancing flecks his vision was back, and he saw the long piece of rusted metal doorframe in Lucas's hands, raised above his head, knew that he was helpless to stop him –

- and was astonished to see his whole body stiffen, as if turned to stone, and fall backwards like a solid plank, to the ground.

He managed to turn his head slightly, and saw Clara standing a few feet away, arms out straight in front of her, both hands on the taser. He smiled, knowing that would be a sight he would cherish for the rest of his life.

THIRTY-FIVE

"I think this will do, yes?" Dina said, looking up from the pages.

"We don't have to set up in any particular part of the house, then?" Ed said, his bag containing the items for the ritual on his shoulder.

"According to these instructions, we must place ourselves in the lowest part of the building we can. This is the cellar. This is right."

They stood side by side at the bottom of the staircase that had led them here from the main hallway of the rectory above. The room was expansive and made entirely of stone, with shallow barrelled ceilings, archways between the three specific areas and slate steps built into various walls for shelving. Wooden barrels, weighted at the bottom, were scattered around, used as tables, wooden chairs around each. Six stone posts, two in each section had been erected, copper lamps hung at the top. Three chain-suspended copper-bowl chandeliers hung from the ceiling, one in each section. Dina flicked the switch on the wall next to her and candleholders replaced by bulbs glowed softly, the obtuse angles of the stonework, creating oblique shadows throughout. The air held the slightest touch of earthiness, and was completely devoid of all sounds from above.

In the centre of the first section, was a long, rectangular table, broken crockery and glassware strewn across it, dust covered. Dried up flower stems lay collapsed over the edge of a china vase in the middle.

At the archway to the second section, the double end-chain for the chandeliers dangled from the winding block to the floor. Beyond it was empty. The third section to the right housed empty walnut wine racks, running around all three walls.

Ed moved to the table and put the bag on it. "Ok, so, what's next?" Ed asked.

Dina read a few lines. "There isn't that much we can do before they arrive with Lucas, but now we can draw the Leviathan cross in the centre of the room using the gold." When they'd read the list sitting in The Pie Chart, gold was one item they thought would prove extremely difficult to get, especially as time was against them. Ed had impressed Dina when, having gone and spoken to the woman behind the counter, he returned a few moments later with a round metal container about the size of a shoe polish tin. She'd given him a very odd look, until he opened it.

"Gold," he'd said grinning. "Twenty-four carat edible gold powder. They use it in baking. I remember my mother, who was an extremely good cook I might add, always thought the idea was ridiculous."

Dina had laughed. "You're not just a pretty face, are you?"

"And I'm not a rich one either," Ed had said. "That just cost me a packet, so you can owe me half."

He now took the same tin out of the bag. "I never asked you, why gold?"

She looked up at him from the papers. "This is not unusual. Gold has been associated with the occult for thousands of years; it symbolises purity, divinity and is supposed to embody the power of kind gods. I hope this is right." Reading again, she then said, "Two lit candles must be placed on the top cross-piece, one on the second and an unlit one of the third."

"I thought the Leviathan cross was thought to be a satanic symbol," Ed said.

"Yes, it is commonly accepted as such, but the Celts knew of it's true meaning, also understood by my father's sect too, of course. The top cross piece represents The Light, the second the Half-Light and the third, The Dark. The infinity symbol at the bottom signifies just that: the layer beneath The Dark is trapped there forever, and must always remain that way."

Ed pulled out the small earthenware bowl they bought from a gift shop. "And this?"

"Hang on," Dina said, reading more. "This is the awkward bit: when Lucas is here, we need a drop of blood from his –," she frowned, ensuring she had the

265

translation correct – "yes, his tongue." She winced. "The ritual requires blood from the tongue of '*he who invited such an abomination forward. This should be given in to an earthen vessel, as Earth is the strongest of the Four Elements and will assist in the opening of the layers.* This is then placed in the middle of the infinity symbol. It looks to me as if we consider the bowl a 'keyhole' and the words of the ritual, as the 'key'. It's hard to make exact sense of this, but I think that is close."

"As long as it works, Dina. Like Alex said, just read it verbatim, and let it do what it does. Help me move this, will you?" He moved to the far side of the table and began pushing it to one side of the room. It was far heavier than it looked, and it took the both of them almost five minutes to get it out of the way. Once done, Ed took the tin of gold dust and carefully began tapping it out on the stone floor, in the shape of a large Leviathan cross.

Once done, Dina placed the candles on each of the cross-pieces, lit the first three as instructed and stood back. "That's it." she said, picking up the bowl and looking at it. "Now, we just need Lucas."

THIRTY-SIX

"Jon from Kyle, receiving?"

"Go on, Kyle,"

"We're about two minutes away. He's in the back, cuffed. Are you there yet?"

"Same ETA for me. Are you okay?"

"Yeah. Both got headaches but that's all. See you there."

Kyle dropped the radio on to his lap. Clara was now driving, the less concussed of the two. Lucas was slumped in the rear, hands cuffed behind his back, face pale, eyes wide. He had not said a word since being unceremoniously bundled into the car, Clara refusing to remove the pins from the taser still stuck in his skin until he was secure. So when he spoke, it surprised both of them.

"Who are you?" His voice was quiet, and full of fear.

"We're here to clear up the God-awful shit storm you've stirred up," Kyle said. "It's irrelevant who we are. We're keeping you alive right now."

The resignation on Lucas's face clear, an instant

understanding that Kyle and Clara somehow knew exactly what had happened. "How did you find out?" he asked.

"Look, mate, I'm not the person to be asking these questions. We'll be at the rectory in a minute – that's where it started, right?" Lucas nodded feebly. "There are people there who'll tell you what's going to happen."

"Do you realise what you've done?" Clara said, dropping a gear and hitting the accelerator hard as the road began to climb. "That people have been seriously hurt?"

"Yes - no - I knew something had gone wrong, but it was an accident. It wasn't what I was trying to do. I tried to stop it. I'm so sorry."

"Do you even know what '*it*' is, Lucas?" Clara said.

Lucas shook his head, his eyes beginning to fill with tears.

"Friends of ours will want to speak to you. Make damn sure you tell them everything they need to know. As well as possibly many others, your own life depends on it."

The road now straightened out, and Clara switched to full beam, mud and gravel kicking up behind them as she floored the accelerator.

"In about half a mile there's a sign for Long Mire and a right turn. Go past it, and take the next one," Kyle said, looking out the rear window. He frowned, held his focus for a second. "It's faster," he said and sat back round.

Thirty seconds later the sign flashed by, and Clara hit the brakes hard, the turn rushing into her headlights sooner than she expected. The car fishtailed a touch as she tore into the lane, but she kept the oversteer shallow. The car straightened, and she hit the pedal again.

They were on the lane for no more than half a mile before she recognised the wall now running along their right side, knew that the old rectory gates would be appearing soon.

She cut her speed, and a hundred feet later, they were there, light from her full beam illuminating the ornate metalwork. She turned in through them, along a short tree-lined drive, and onto the gravel frontage of Long Mire Rectory, where Dina's mini was parked.

Even in its state of abandonment, it was still a building that left an impression. At each end were pointed eaves, double windows on the first floor level of each, and a window in-between the two structures. Along the whole front of the house ran a brick veranda with iron arch work and a fence of complimentary design around the bottom. Six large sash windows peered out from under the veranda, once allowing streams of sunlight into what had been a lively and happy place, but it had lain empty now for more than fifty years.

As Clara pulled up, headlights suddenly appeared behind her, a second later Jon's unmarked and Angus's Land Rover pulling up sharply, gravel spitting up around the tyres. The two men came running over to their car as Clara and Kyle got out. The wind that had got steadily stronger over the last few days now brought with it the start of rain: large, heavy drops, as cold as the night itself.

"Are you guys alright?" Angus asked, the gale snatching at his words, making them harder to hear.

"We're fine, Dad. Let's get Lucas in. He's not great."

Kyle opened the door, fighting the wind for possession and helped Lucas out, Angus and Jon taking an arm each as he stood clear of the car. They wasted no time getting inside, but as Kyle went to close the front door, he took another look outside, long enough for Clara to ask him what he was waiting for.

"I think I might need my eyes testing," he said obtusely, then shut it.

Jon took out his radio, keeping hold of Lucas. "Ed, where are you guys?"

"In the cellar. Take the stairs in the main hallway on the right."

"Angus, it might be an idea if you up stay here, keep an eye out for any unwanted visitors," Jon said. "I know it's unlikely, but until we at least get things started, I'd rather be safe than sorry."

"Ok," Angus said. "Wise idea."

Jon looked at Lucas. "Are you alright, nipper?"

"I'm so sorry. I never meant for anything like this to happen."

"Yeah, we know. Just do what you're asked, and we have a chance to put an end to all this." He motioned toward the stairs. "Come on," he said.

Angus let go of Lucas's arm, and Jon, holding him by the cuffs, let him take the stairs first and followed, Kyle and Clara behind him. When they reached the cellar, they found Dina sat at one of the barrel tables adjacent to the one of the stone posts, pouring over the papers, Ed bent down next to the Leviathan cross lighting the candles.

"This is Lucas Crane, Dina," Jon said, walking him over to the table. He sat Lucas down, and took the chair next to him.

"Lucas, my name is Dina Melnyk. I am a doctor of occult studies at De Havilland University. This is Ed Thorne, a paranormal investigator, and the man whose cuff's you are wearing is Sergeant Jon Pearce. Kyle and Clara who brought you here are friends of ours, and we are all here to send back the Zalyshky layer you unleashed."

Lucas shook his head. "What is it? I don't know what I did, or what I summoned up. I don't know anything about it."

"That does not matter," Dina said. "What did you do when you first came here?"

"I wanted to contact the spirit world, to prove there really is life after death, that's all."

"That's all?" Dina said. "That is stupidity of the highest order, and where do you gain your expertise from, Lucas?"

"I – well, I don't have expertise. I teach myself. From

books. From TV."

"Yes – stupidity and ignorance. Not a good combination in any field of study, but particularly dangerous when dealing with the occult, but this is not the time to be telling you this. How did you try to contact the spirit world?"

"I used a Ouija board. Nothing special. I just came here a few times and tried to get it to work."

"How many times?"

"I don't know…four or five, maybe?"

"You had four or five sessions? That would not have been enough to do any damage."

"Four or five days."

"In a row?" Lucas nodded. "And how many sessions each of those days?"

"I don't know. Honestly, I don't, but I was here for the whole evening each time."

Dina ran a hand through her hair and looked at the others. "That would certainly do it."

"Do what?" Lucas asked, his voice stating to break up. "What did I do?"

"It is unlikely you carried out these Ouija sessions correctly, as you do not know what you are doing. And each time you did this, you weakened the barrier between this and the spirit world, very seriously and you did this so often over those four days, you weakened it enough in this place for a strain of Zalyshky to escape up through the layers and into this world. You didn't summon it, but you did enable it."

"What is Zalyshky?" Dina explained it as briefly as she could, watching Lucas as she did so, his eyes beginning to bulge, and his lips tremble.

"Oh my God! Is it going to possess me? Please don't let it, Dina, please."

"It does not want your body, Lucas. It is what's inside you, that which gives you life itself that it wants. It wants to become fully sentient." She looked him in the eye. "It wants to be alive."

"So what's going to happen to me?" He was starting to weep.

"Nothing, because we are here to stop it. But if we were not, it would drain you of your life, simply that. You would die. It has been strongly attracted to your life source since you gave it the means to break through, and has been trying to find you ever since, leaving chaos and agony in its wake. It has left this place untouched – it does not want to damage the gateway it has used, but everywhere you have been there is destruction. This is its nature. It is not even something it tries to do – it just happens wherever it has been."

"I knew something had gone wrong. On one of the last sessions I did, the room began to grow darker, and I could hear what sounded like a child's scream. It scared the living shit out of me and I just ran."

Dina nodded. "We know you have been recently to the museum, the vets and Will's place. Have you been to the beach and the church? St Michael?

Lucas nodded feebly. "I tried to draw a Celtic rune

trap in the old cemetery, but the old bloke, the one who got buried, I saw him so I ran off. I saw his picture in the paper. They said it was an accident."

"No, this is untrue," Dina said, "What about the church?"

"I just wanted to be somewhere safe for a while."

"Have you felt unwell in the last few days? Fatigued, sick?"

"Only since this morning, but it came on really quickly. I've puked a couple of times, and felt very weak. It's got worse since you found me, too."

"Lucas, Zalyshky has been tracking you – irresistibly following the living energy you put out as you go, much like a human scent to a dog. It gets nearer and nearer, catching up with you, and now that you are feeling its effects, it must be very near. Close enough to begin draining you of that eternal essence. If it helps to make it sound less 'sci-fi', the Chinese, Tibetans, Japanese, and many more have believed strongly in its existence for hundreds of years: Chi, Ki, Aura, Qi call it what you like. It exists in all of us, and Zalyshky wants yours - and is close to getting it."

Tears were now pouring down Lucas's face. "How are you going to stop it? You can definitely stop it, can't you?" he pleaded.

"We've had help from people with expert knowledge. They have given us instructions and we need to carry them out to the letter."

"What'll happen when you do this? What'll happen

to *me*?"

Dina shrugged her shoulders, no attempt to hide the gesture. "I do not know, Lucas. I have never done this before. None of us have, but my father did this many times, and I believe you'll be safe." She touched his arm once more. "I will not let Zalyshky take you."

The tension in the room was palpable, but with a loud static that cut through the air, Angus's voice came through.

"Jon, I'm coming down. The rust, and all that other shit, it's creeping across all the metal and woodwork up here. It's just started, so that bloody thing must be here."

"Ed," Dina said, she said gesturing towards Lucas. "His tongue." Lucas turned to look at Ed, horror on his face. "What the hell are you doing?" he said as the investigator fished out his Leatherman and came towards him.

Angus bowled into the room from the stairway, came to a grinding halt as he saw the proceedings in front of him.

"We need blood from your tongue. I'm sorry but there's no way around this."

"No! No way," Lucas screamed trying to move away but Jon caught his cuffs and pulled him to a standstill.

"I'm not cutting it out, for Christ sake," Ed said, "just a tiny nick. Do you want to die?"

"No, no."

"Then open your mouth," Ed said, taking out the shortest blade on the penknife. "This is making me feel sick, Lucas, so I'm certainly not enjoying this either."

Lucas opened his mouth just a centimetre, as if it wouldn't move anymore.

"Lucas!" Ed shouted and the young man opened wider. Ed held his jaw. "Now keep still," he said, and with as quick and short a movement as he could, he drew the point of the knife across the tip of his tongue. Lucas cried out, and pulled his head back involuntarily, his hands struggling to come to his face despite being cuffed.

Ed grabbed the bowl, and shoved it in front of his face. "Spit," he commanded. Lucas did as was told, and dribble of blood dripped into the vessel. He spat again, phlegm mixing with the blood this time, creating a stingy trail from his lips to the bowl.

"That'll do," Dina said, "put it on the middle of the infinity symbol, quickly." Ed did so, then went to stand next to her.

The room fell completely silent as Dina prepared to start reciting the ritual, and all heads tiled back as from above, the strange grating, crackling sound became apparent, moving along the room, towards the stairway.

"That bloody thing is getting really close," Angus said.

"The stairs," Ed shouted, Clara and Kyle instinctively jumping up and moving away. They all looked, and at the very top, the light seemed to have been extinguished by deep shadow that moved slowly downward toward them.

"I knew I'd seen something," Kyle said. "When we were in the car talking to Lucas, I thought I saw something in the road behind us. It seemed to be blocking out the hedges and road as it came towards us, but I thought it was my imagination. It looked like – like that thing," he said nodding towards the stairs.

Clara grabbed Kyle's hand and together with her father, skirted around the cross and stood next to the other stone pillar, and Dina who began reading aloud the Russian incantation before her.

Nothing happened, and already, they could see the Zalyshky strain darkening more of the stair.

Dina read on, loud and strong, and then –

- it all began.

The gold of the top cross-piece began to glow, then undulate as if suddenly liquid. Within a second, amongst an explosion of hissing and spitting it phosphoresced, and like a ravenous fuse, the reaction passed down and onto the second cross-piece. As it reached the third, the air in the room had turned astonishingly fresh and cool, as if they were now standing on a high summit. The pressure changed rapidly, everyone's ears popping.

"The element of Air has been invoked, I believe," Dina said above the hissing of the gold. "The page says I have to stop here and wait for it to '*peel back the face*', whatever that is."

"Why Air?" Jon said.

"It's the element of movement, fluidity, the motion

of all things," Ed said. "It could be playing a part in the barrier between us and the spirit realm falling away."

Jon opened his mouth to speak but was immediately cut off as from the cross itself, a wind of ferocious strength erupted. It hit the ceiling, brickwork, and stone, itself caught in the wind and sent hurling outwards beyond the room. As the speeding air rushed over their heads, it gripped hair and skin, distorting their faces, but seeming to leave everyone's balance undisturbed. It pulled at every part of everyone's head and neck, causing cheeks to billow and eyes lids to tighten, and as pain started to mount –

-it was gone.

In its stead, the air remained cool and its pressure low, and there was now a continuous humming sound, so deep, it actually vibrated in their chests.

"I'd say that was the 'face peeling bit', wouldn't you?" Ed said.

"Okay," Dina agreed and once again, began reading the ritual from where she had left off.

The line of enflamed gold had reached the vessel at the centre of the infinity symbol, and as it struck, the bowl exploded into dust, but the drops of Lucas's blood remained there, suspended as if in zero gravity. Dina read on, raising her voice further, and the drops began to coagulate into one globule. It then slowly descended, the deep hum increasing in strength, and as it touched the centre of the infinity symbol, like hot steel poured into a clean mould, the blood swept around and filled the shape perfectly, any unburnt dust falling away. At the same time, the fire across the gold extinguished with a single 'crack' that echoed throughout the cellar – and all at once, there was no sound other than Dina's voice and the deep hum.

Jon turned Lucas around and took off the cuffs. "If there comes a time when the only thing left to do is run, then run," he said quietly. "Because, trust me, I'll be a hundred metres ahead of you."

"I have to stop reading here again," Dina said. "This time to wait for *'the faces of God's children who are contented and so are brief, the pleas of the Deniers whom we must not allow to covet us or take our hand, for the cries of those in The Dark who we must strike away and repel. Then must you continue with vigour resolute.'*" She looked at Ed. "If you see before I do when I should start reading again, for Christ's sake tell me."

Ed went to answer, but instead, his jaw remained open, his eyes looking up above her head. Everyone was doing the same, and she turned, following their gaze.

The hum had vanished. Behind and a few feet above her, the shape of a face had begun to materialise, as if pressing through a beautifully fine gauze of pure, white light. It hung there, and though the features were not defined, more undulation than shape, it was clear its eyes were moving, looking around the room, a smile of serene joy shaping its lips. Then, another began to appear on the opposite side of the room, an entirely

280

different face but with the same searching eyes and a smile that was full of peace. Within seconds there were more, and within a minute, enough to fill the entire room, some randomly fading as others appeared. Everyone could feel the overwhelming sense of grace and peace around them, of a sudden innate knowledge that something astonishingly tranquil and divine was with them.

"*The faces of God's children*," Jon said with utter astonishment, unable to take his eyes from the sublime faces before him.

"The layers have started to open," Dina gasped. "They have actually started to open right in front of us."

"Spirits who have passed into The Light," Ed said. "They must be." But as he finished his words, more and more began to fade, with no more appearing to replace them.

"*Contented and brief*, right?" Jon said, his voice slightly broken.

Ed nodded. "I suppose so."

Everyone continued to look high around the room, and a moment later, Kyle pointed at a space just in front of the chandeliers.

"There," he said.

In the same way as the faces of light had begun to appear, so did the those by the chandelier – only this time, it was as if the gauze that slipped across their features was made of dark pearl. The eyes of each still searched the room, but they were half closed, drawn down at the edges, and their lips so forlorn, no one in the room could help but feel tears in their eyes, a feeling of such heavy sadness in their chests.

Then arms and hands began to appear, reaching down to them, their expression pleading with them to take hold, to bring them back in to the world.

"They must be those in the Half-Light," Dina said. "Unable to accept their deaths, or wanting to return to the living to attend unfinished business."

"Don't touch them, no matter how strong the compulsion," Ed said to everyone. "The last thing we need are anymore entities crossing over."

As no one responded to the outstretched arms, they heard the moans begin – incoherent at first, then forming the word – 'please' – over and over again, the voices no more than whispers. Clara looked down at the floor, unable to meet the gaze of the sorrowful faces, fingers in her ears, but it was not long before they, too, began to fade away.

"It will be a glimpse into The Dark layer next," Dina said. "Don't do anything. Nothing from there can come across to us if we don't interact. We are just seeing the layers parting."

No one said anything, everyone bracing themselves for The Dark and it came almost immediately. Again, faces appearing, some human, others something entirely different, their features black, almost like liquid tar as deceitful and insidious eyes scoured the room, grimaces and distorted lips sending out waves of pain and suffering. Everyone kept their eyes away, even when the guttural snarls and stuttering screeches began, the long, high screams and the foul, rasping laughter. And as that faded, driven away by everyone's refusal to react, Ed laid a hand on Dina's shoulder and said calmly - "Now."

"I think so too," she said and for the third time, began reading again, ensuring her voice was clear and forceful.

After a few sentences, as at the beginning –

- nothing happened.

She read on, and still –

-nothing.

After another paragraph, without any kind of warning, the sphere materialised instantaneously. It hung in the centre of the room, sixteen feet across, spinning at great velocity, directly above the Leviathan cross, it's gravity strong enough such that everyone had to work hard not to be immediately dragged a few feet forward. Kyle wrapped his arm around the stone post, holding Clara tight with the other. Angus reached out and grasped the chandelier chain hanging down the wall.

The sphere emitted no noise, but its mass was so fathomless, the very depth of the black that created it so intense, it was like looking straight into a burning sun.

Dina almost stopped reading, so stunned by it, but she focused hard, and carried on, almost shouting now.

"Jesus Christ," Ed said. "I think we're actually looking into Zalyshky itself."

"But more of it can't come though?" Jon asked.

"No, no," Ed said. "We're looking into that layer. Nothing has been summoned; Dina has kept to the reading word for word. I think the layers have been parted and we're being given access to Zalyshky, but not the other way around. At least I bloody-well hope not, or we're all screwed."

Dina was reading faster now, intently and after two lines, the sphere began to rotate at phenomenal speed, at once the gravitational pull increasing ten-fold. With a strange, far-distance noise akin to a child's scream, the stairway filled with the dark matter, the Zalyshky strain, as it was pulled violently towards the sphere. It almost came to a stop but as Dina continued to read, once again, and with another distant scream, it was dragged forward, suddenly gathering speed, as the front of it was sucked into the sphere.

At the same time, everyone's legs were swept from underneath them – Angus gripped the chain with both arms, Kyle hooked his elbow harder around the pilar and Clara yelled out, slamming her other hand on to his wrist, holding hard with both. Jon slid forward into one of the barrels, Ed slipped six feet but managed to grab a leg of the large table, and Dina and Lucas bundled in behind him, his body stopping them being dragged any further.

Lucas screamed, and threw his arms around Ed's waist. Dina reached back and hooked an arm around the other table leg, still gripping on tightly to the papers in her other hand. Ed used both arms to pull himself closer to the table leg, hooked his elbow around it, then reached down to grab Lucas's wrist.

Dina gritted her teeth, pulling her hand towards her, so she could see the last few words of the ritual and with the very first word it happened –

- as if something was trying to pull his bones out through his skin, parts of Lucas's body began to bulge outwards as they were pulled towards the sphere, skin stretching hideously. He screamed, but the sound distorted, suddenly low, then high again, a croaking, grating sound. In a second, his skin was white, and his hair began to tear from its scalp, along with bits of his clothes.

Dina looked appalled, and stammered.

"Don't stop!" Ed shouted.

"The strain is still trying to take his life source from him," Dina cried. "For God's sake don't let go of him, Ed."

"I won't – keep reading, keep reading."

Dina continued and the childlike scream came again, as the strain was pulled further into the sphere, but it would not give up – for the most fleeting chance to feel what it meant to be alive, no matter how brief – it *could* not give up.

More of Dina's words and the sphere's velocity increased yet again.

Cries went up as the increase in the gravitational pull tore at their arms and elbows. Another heart-breaking scream came from Lucas's, as his eyes began protruding from their sockets towards the sphere, then his cheeks and lips, his neck, stomach, and down until the whole front of his body was bowed outward as the strain continued to tear at his very being, this time an aura of stunning bright white, the entire length and width of his body, seeming to extrude from him. Ed growled in pain as his fingers strained to keep hold of him, but with Lucas's gripping back so hard, he seemed to have him securely.

"That's it," Dina said. "There's no more to read. The strain is being pulled in, returning to its origin. Can you keep hold of him for a few more seconds, Ed?"

"I think so," Ed said – just as the sphere began to spin even faster.

"Kyle!" Clara screamed, "I'm slipping. I can't hold on."

"You let go of her and I'll kill you myself, Kyle," bellowed Angus, fighting the gravitational pull, trying to get to them both, his hands beginning to slip down the chain.

"I'm trying, I'm trying," Kyle hollered back, trying to bury his fingers into Clara's very skin.

"I can't get to her," Jon shouted. The second I move either side of this barrel I'm straight into that sphere."

"Kyle! Dad!" Clara cried, "I can't hold on."

"Just a few seconds more," Dina shouted across to them.

"I'm slipping, I don't have any grip," Clara cried out. "Kyle, please don't let me go, please!"

"Kyle, please, don't let her go," Angus cried, the agony in his voice heart rending. "Hold on, just a few more seconds!"

"Oh, God, no," Ed said, dread suddenly in his voice. "My hands are getting numb. I can't feel them."

The scream cut through the mayhem again, as the strain tore at Lucas, but the sphere began to spin even faster, and this time it was too much –

– Kyle bawled in horror, as he felt Clara's fingers slip over his wrist and he lost her.

She flew through the air, Angus crying out in anguish but at the very same time, Lucas's scream overpowered every other noise, his body already in the air a few feet ahead of Clara, and both he and the strain were immediately engulfed by the sphere.

Instantaneously the black sun vanished, Clara hit the floor, and the sudden silence was absolute. A second or two later, Ed used the table leg and pulled himself up. He turned to everyone, his head shaking.

"I'm so sorry. I couldn't hold him any longer," he said. "I thought I had him. I'm so sorry."

Everyone picked themselves up, and Dina took his hand.

"You did all you could, Ed."

Angus and Kyle ran over to see if Clara was okay. She lay still, breathing heavily. "If you weren't such a weakling, Ed, I wouldn't be here now," she said, trying a smile to reassure him, but not quite making it. "Thank you." she said, meeting his eyes, deep sincerity in her own.

Jon came up to Ed, laid a hand on his shoulder. Ed nodded a little, ran his hand through his hair. "I need a very large drink," he said quietly. "Anyone else?"

THIRTY-SEVEN

Jon and Dina had scrubbed away the Leviathan cross, and dusty remains of the bowl with their feet, and put the candles and gold powder back in the bag. Other than that, there was nothing to indicate that anything other than time and abandonment had affected the room.

"Did that really happen?" Angus said. "I know that must be the most stupid thing I've said in my life, but standing here now - this room, it's just a cellar. The quiet. It seems unreal."

"Nothing like a glimpse into hell itself to change your outlook on life, right?" Kyle said, eyes fixed in the middle distance.

Dina was bent, picking up the pages and Ed came over to her.

"Here," he said, handing the match he had used for the candles to Dina.

She took them without saying a word, flicked the flint, and touched the flame to the edge of the papers. They burned without fuss, like any old copy paper would. Within a minute, they were ashes on the floor.

"Is everyone okay?" Jon asked. There were nods, but no words. "Sure?" he asked again; mumbled agreement.

"How do we deal with Lucas?" Ed said.

"I'll put the ferry reservation slip back in his bedroom. He'll get treated as a missing person when someone finally reports it but that could be some time. The checks we ran showed no next of kin, and I doubt he had any close friends on the island." He shook his head. "I know this was all necessary. We had no choice. We couldn't stand by and let countless others suffer like Frank and the others, but I still can't believe I'm planting evidence."

"You're returning it, Jon, not planting it," Dina said.

"I suppose so." He thought for a moment. "Maybe Nic will report it when he notices Lucas hasn't been in for a few weeks?"

"We should go now," Dina said. "There is no point in staying here any longer."

"Let's get back to Will's, get some alcohol inside us. We can at least tell him it's over," Jon said.

"In as little detail as possible?" Ed suggested.

Dina nodded. "This is right, Ed." She started towards the stairway, everyone following, but as she reached the foot, she turned, looked at everyone in turn.

"And I'm sure it goes without saying," she said, "that none of this ever – *ever* - goes beyond this room."

THIRTY-EIGHT

The sky was cloudless, a perfect powder blue, and for the time of year, the sun was surprisingly warm. Jon and Ed could see Dina standing on the rear deck, watching them, and as the ferry began to pull away, she waved. They waved back, and watched for a while longer, before turning and heading back to the car.

"Are you really going to retire?" Ed asked.

"Been thinking about it a long time. This has changed everything for me. I'm still trying to get my head around it all - what we saw - the *ramifications* of what we saw. There's so much going on in my head, but if there's anything that has really hit me, it's made me realise I need to do the things I want to before it's too late. Live this life I have, rather than just existing."

Ed nodded slowly; eyes fixed on the horizon for a moment. Then he said, "You know the money in my line of work is pretty crap, don't you? But after this, I've realised I need someone like you to keep me on my toes. Going forward after what we went through, I don't think I can do this kind of work on my own anymore."

"Really?" Jon said. "I could be up for that - but only if I get to be the EMF bloke."

Ed sucked in air through clenched teeth, feigning concern. "Hmm. We'll have to negotiate on that. Scaring the crap out of you every time that thing went off was the highlight of this case."

"Idiot," Jon said.

Ed laughed quietly. "Any idea how Clara and Kyle will deal with this?"

"Clara will accept it fully; I do know that. She's been into all the paranormal stuff for years, so for her, I imagine it's a huge vindication of her study and beliefs. She'll be thrilled, I imagine. As for Kyle, what he sees he takes as read, if I know him right. He won't talk about it to anyone, he won't want to be taken for an idiot. But he'll know what he saw, and be satisfied with that."

For a few moments, they sat in silence listening to the sea lapping against the dock walls.

Eventually Ed said, "How do you think Angus will take to Clara and Kyle being an item, then?"

"They're not yet, as far as I know," Jon said.

"It won't be long."

Jon gave a sideways smile. "She's a grown woman. She knows what she's doing, and she doesn't suffer fools gladly. And she can handle her dad."

"Good for them," Ed said.

They reached the unmarked and got in. "If you could help me round up my gear, that would great. I can get packed and be on my way later this evening. If we stop off somewhere I'll get Will a decent bottle of whisky."

"What about Dina?" Jon asked.

Ed shook his head. "That, I honestly don't know. She's a strange one, Dina. I've known her for years, but there's still a lot I don't know about her. She doesn't show her feelings, and most of the time, keeps her opinions very much to herself." He nodded briefly. "I'll call her tomorrow. See how she is."

"Let me know," Jon said and started the engine.

"How about a last blue light run? I'm never going to get the chance again after this."

"It's not strictly legal. We're not attending a call," Jon said, thought there was a lack of conviction in his voice.

"Dull," Ed said.

"Okay then, I'll ask you a question, and *only* if I believe you're telling me the truth, I'll give you a final blue lighter."

"Deal."

Jon paused a moment, then looking straight ahead through the windscreen he said, "Did you honestly lose your grip on Lucas?" He then turned and looked at his friend.

Ed looked back at him. "Yes," he said.

A second later, Jon pulled away smoothly, sticking precisely to the 30mph speed limit as they drove off towards the town.

THIRTY-NINE

The Reaching Tree was one of Ed's favourite comfort stops on the way back from anywhere in the north. The car park was only big enough for three cars, and he'd never seen anyone else here in the three years he'd be using it.

The tree itself stood just back from the front edge of the place, its bark-stripped, smooth trunk reaching up less than ten feet before it curved almost ninety degrees, ending in four gnarled branches, as if reaching out for something that had long since slipped its grasp.

The sun set behind it, and on an evening such as this, it backlit the expanse of broken clouds, giving them a halo of soft white and lending everything else at once, an iridescent glow and deep shadow on all that was east facing.

Ed sat back, opened his flask and poured himself a coffee, the steam immediately clouding his windscreen for a moment. For the entire drive so far, he had tried to find any reason possible to dismiss the deep excitement lodged in his chest. What he had seen *was* real. Of course it was bloody real. Which meant he had finally found what he had been searching for all his life. So many years of either nothing, or morsels of evidence he couldn't substantiate. And in the space of five days, all the answers he had been seeking were thrust in front of his very eyes.

It was astounding to him that he might now be able to find her again. So utterly astounding that he still couldn't stop his mind trying to come up with reasons why that was impossible.

But he had to use this new knowledge to try. After all this time, he really had nothing at all to lose.

He held the warm cup in his hands, and with a wide smile, as the sun continued to set, he watched beautiful shadows develop across the vast carpet of pink rhododendrons that surrounded The Reaching Tree.

FORTY

As the evening drew in, the clement change in the weather brought with it a warm breeze which scuttled around the broken windows and old air vents of the rectory. Trees along the driveway swayed gently against a dark-navy sky, stars beautifully clear, the light from The Lend doing little to spoil the clarity.

Inside, the breeze danced across the hallway, through empty doorways and down into the cellar, and in the very far corner it found something to tug at, jammed under a barrel as if driven there by some powerful force: a piece of paper, the corner poking out from underneath.

It fluttered as the breeze teased it out, bit by bit, determined to have its prize.

Then, quite suddenly, it was free, lifting into the air, circling for a while, it's photocopied content blurred by the gloom, before floating back down, and coming to rest in the middle of the floor…